WHISPERING CITY

PREVIOUS WORKS BY THE SAME AUTHOR

Murder in the Rough

(Published under "Leslie Allen")
The Corpse was a Blonde
Doom Over America

TO BE PUBLISHED

The Town
Murder A La Carte

Whispering City

A Study in Suspense

ADAPTED BY

Horace Brown

FROM THE

Quebec Productions' Film
based on an original story by
George Zuckerman and Michael Lennox

A
Ricochet
Book

Véhicule Press

Published with the generous assistance of the Canada Council
for the Arts and the Canada Book Fund of the Department
of Canadian Heritage.

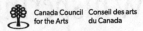

Canada Council   Conseil des arts
for the Arts   du Canada

Canadä

RICOCHET SERIES EDITOR: BRIAN BUSBY
Adaptation of original cover: Brian Morgan
Special assistance: Julie Jacques
Typeset in Minion and Greenstone by Simon Garamond
Printed by Marquis Printing

Published by Véhicule Press, Montréal, Québec, Canada
www.vehiculepress.com

Distribution in Canada by LitDistCo
www.litdistco.ca

Distribution in the USA by Independent Publishers Group
www.ipgbook.com

Printed in Canada on FSC®-certified paper

MIX
Paper from
responsible sources
FSC® C103567

INTRODUCTION

This is a story straight out of Hollywood. It begins with a plot laid down by George Zuckerman and Michael Lennox, then fleshed out and made into a screenplay by Rian James and Leonard Lee. A dark thriller, it was supposed to be set in New York, but the resulting film, *Whispering City*, takes place in Old Quebec.

The relocation northward was the doing of Paul L'Anglais, co-founder of the newly-formed Quebec Productions Corporation. Born and raised in Quebec City, L'Anglais had intended to become a lawyer, but instead ended up as one of Canadian radio's earliest and most successful directors and producers. *Whispering City* marked his entrée to film production. L'Anglais' had several novel ideas, one of which involved making two movies simultaneously: one in English, the other in French. Each scene would be shot twice, often with one cast waiting off-camera to replace the other.

Work on both *Whispering City* and *La Forteresse*, its French-language sister, began in August of 1946. The following spring, the former was screened for critics. Ron Gadsby of the Canadian Press filed a most enthusiastic wire story:

> Something new has been added to the celluloid
> art. Something new, something fine, something
> Canadian. Who said we couldn't make movies?

Whispering City is something Canadian, but it is not *wholly* Canadian. Zuckerman, Lennox, James and Lee were Americans. Director Fedor Ozep – Fyodor Aleksandrovich Otsep – was a Russian exile. Where the leading roles were performed by Quebec *vedettes* Nicole Germain, Paul Dupuis, and Jacques Auger in *La Forteresse*, L'Anglais chose Hollywood actors Mary Anderson, Helmut Dantine, and Paul Lukas for *Whispering City*.

Still, Ron Gadsby's enthusiasm is understandable. With a combined budget of $600,000 – the final figure is thought to be more than $750,000 – *Whispering City* and *La Forteresse* were by far the most expensive Canadian films ever made. They were unlike any previous features in that they depicted an urban Canada; one populated not by lumberjacks, farmers, and Mounties, rather musicians, lawyers, judges, journalists, and street-smart police detectives. Key to the plot is the performance of the *Concerto de Québec* by seventeen-year-old André Mathieu, a musical protégé who was being touted as the first great Canadian composer.

Whispering City and *La Forteresse* are this country's earliest examples of *film noir*, and yet both buck convention. A woman plays the lead. Mary Roberts – Marie Roberts in *La Forteresse* – is a crime reporter, working at a time in which her sex was all but relegated to the Women's page. As a cigarette-smoking, sharply-dressed, independent career woman who lives on her own, she is unlike other female characters of French Canadian film to that point.

Whispering City has its failings; even Gadsby acknowledges "minor flaws." To this critic, its great failing lies in not embracing the titular city with its narrow, winding, climbing, confusing maze of lanes and streets. All too often Ozep shoots during the daytime in bright open spaces which in no way reflect the mood being sought. Six years later, Alfred Hitchcock would use the city to greater effect with *I Confess*. Interestingly, in the preface of this novelization, Horace Brown references the master, writing that *Whispering City* "has moments

Présente
LA FORTERESSE

PAUL DUPUIS · NICOLE GERMAIN · JACQUES AUGER

of Hitchcock suspense against a background to be found nowhere else in the world."

There have not been many novelizations of Canadian films – I believe the most recent was the curling comedy *Men with Brooms* (2002) – and so it may seem cheap praise to describe Horace Brown's effort as the best. While the genre was not in its infancy – the earliest examples date back to the silent era – in 1947 books like *Whispering City* were still uncommon; the six-figure print-runs of, say, *Battle for the Planet of the Apes* (1973) were the stuff of an unimaginable future.

In his preface, Brown remarks on the challenge of writing the adaptation: "It is not often an author has the privilege of taking a moving-picture (cinema, if you prefer), and turning it into a book. The process is usually reversed."

Horace Brown had another concern in that the novelization came from his own company, Global Publishing. A short-lived firm located in Pickering, Ontario, it began with the pulp magazines *All-New Western Stories* and *Original Detective Stories*. Global published only three books – *Henry V*, *Great Expectations*, and *Whispering City* – all of which were designed to capitalize on recent cinematic releases. *Henry V* and *Great Expectations* reproduce the original texts (with some abridgement); *Whispering City* was the only novelization.

In taking a moving-picture and turning it into a book, Brown sticks close to James and Lee's screenplay, though there are departures. He improves on the dialogue and wisely does away with the chatty sleigh driver who introduces the film. Mary Roberts is given a backstory as an American journalist who had begun her career writing for a New York tabloid. One memorable scene, not featured in the film, has Mary discussing Cornelius Krieghoff, A.Y. Jackson, Tom Thomson, and other Canadian painters with lawyer André Frédéric.

The greatest change involves the villain, who is depicted as a more sinister and threatening figure – clearly a psychopath – adding another coat of *noir*.

Though Brown was not yet forty when he wrote *Whispering City*, he was very much an old pro. A former newspaperman, Brown had been a frequent contributor to magazines in Canada and the United States. He had written dozens of dramas aired on CBC Radio. Boris Karloff had twice read Brown's 'Resurrection' on *The Royal Gelatin Hour*.

And then there were his books.

Whispering City lists three PREVIOUS WORKS BY THE SAME AUTHOR – that author being the pubisher himself:

> *Murder in the Rough*, a story of homicide on the golf course, was published under the *nom de plume*, Leslie Allen.
> *The Corpse Was a Blonde*, another murder mystery, involves beautiful but dead Rita Salton, dope pedlars, and a second corpse (this one a brunette).
> *Doom Over America*, the third of the previous works, is a different sort of mystery. To date, no copy has been found.

Two works, *The Town* and *Murder A La Carte*, are TO BE PUBLISHED. The latter was rewritten and appeared three years later as a cheap News Stand Library paperback titled *The Penthouse Killings*.

The Town is something else altogether. It had been runner-up in the 1945 $1000 Longmans, Green & Company Prize Novel competition, losing to *Darkly the River Flows*, "a Canadian story of strong characters locked in a bitter family conflict" by Lieutenant Commander John Macdonald.

Brown considered *The Town* his greatest work.

It may just be that.

According to Brown, judge B.K. Sandwell, editor of *Saturday Night*, considered *The Town* the best Canadian novel he had ever read. It was self-published in 1977 under the title *Hilary Randall: The Story of The Town*. My copy is inscribed to an employee of Ontario Hydro at which Brown worked at the end of his writing career.

In the preface to *Whispering City*, Brown describes L'Anglais' effort as "the very first Canadian film of importance." Those words would not have met much opposition from the press. Ron Gadsby's praise was in no way unique. Its most enthusiastic supporter was the *Globe & Mail's* Roly Young, who it must be noted, was one of seven newspapermen invited to act in the film.

Whispering City played across Canada and in the United States as *Crime City* (unfair, I think, as it features only one criminal), but it fell short of commercial expectations. Paul L'Anglais' next productions, more modest, focussed exclusively on the Quebec market. In 1951, recognizing the steadily increasing glow of television's cathode ray, he left film production. Quebec Productions closed shop the following year and *Whispering City* fell into the public domain. In the years that followed, "the very first Canadian film of importance" came to be something relegated to reference books. It had a revival, of sorts, with the sort of cheap Beta, VHS, and DVD reissues sold in dollar stores. Muddy prints can be found streaming – *gratis* – online.

Brown's novelization has been nowhere near so accessible. A fragile paperback, it had a modest print run and limited distribution. As of this writing, the lone copy listed for sale online is priced at over three hundred Canadian dollars.

This is a damn shame.

Brown's *Whispering City* is superior to the film, bringing more character and more of this country to what began as an American story.

Paul L'Anglais made *Whispering City* something Canadian.

Horace Brown made it Canadian *noir*.

BRIAN BUSBY is Ricochet Books' series editor. He is the author of over a dozen books, including *Character Parts: Who's Really Who in CanLit*, *A Gentleman of Pleasure: One Life of John Glassco, Poet, Memoirist, Translator, and Pornographer*, and *The Dusty Bookcase: A Journey Through Canada's Forgotten, Neglected and Suppressed Writing*.

PREFACE

It is not often an author has the privilege of taking a moving-picture (cinema, if you prefer), and turning it into a book. The process is usually reversed. Also, the necessity of treating a half-million dollar property with respect is rather conducive to writing jitters. This is complicated when the film in question is a suspense mystery, for the camera can gloss over many things readers will not accept from an author. Too, the camera can pinpoint an emotion with an expression of the face or a significant bit of scenery in a few seconds, where the author must sometimes take pages to reach the same effect.

As a Canadian author with a great and abiding pride in my country, I was faced with another problem. *Whispering City* is not only a six hundred thousand dollar investment; it is also the first Canadian-produced film of consequence and with any pretensions to a world market. It is good cinema. When the difficulties encountered in its making are considered, it is magnificent. It will be, say critics who have previewed the film, a distinct credit to Canada, and the forerunner of even more successful productions to come. This poses a responsibility upon the author I hope I have met.

The Canadian producers of "Whispering City" did not make the mistake of despising experience. René Germain, the French-speaking Canadian financier, backed his judgment of Paul L'Anglais, the brilliant Canadian radio and stage producer, with something as important as money: he gave L'Anglais carte blanche. L'Anglais turned to Hollywood and New York for his story and his technicians. But he did so with a definite purpose in mind. For every American technician who worked on the filming of "Whispering City" at the former naval barracks in Ste. Hyacinthe, thirty miles from Montreal, Quebec, a Canadian stood by to learn. When Quebec Productions make their next film, this policy will pay dividends to 100% Canadian technical personnel.

The film-going public having been educated (perhaps wrongly) to consider the players in the picture more important than the story or the photography, it was necessary that "Whispering City" have "names". From Hollywood and New York, Monsieur L'Anglais imported the veteran actor and Academy award winner, Paul Lukas, and gave him Helmut Dantine, of stage and screen, and darkly beautiful Mary Anderson as his co-stars. Most of the beautiful interiors were shot at Ste. Hyacinthe, and have a rare quality of authenticity. To a former newspaperman like myself, this is particularly marked in the cityroom scenes, which reminded me of nothing so much as the usual morgue-like calm of the cityroom of the *Ottawa Citizen*, where I once worked, and so far removed from the Hollywood conception of a newspaper as to be a refreshing delight. I suspect the scene in the Chateau Frontenac dining-room was actually shot in that famous hostelry, as were the scenes in the Palais de Justice, but I may be wrong. At least, they have the flavor of being real. Exterior scenes were filmed in Quebec City and at Montmorency Falls. Great crowds apparently gathered for the shootings.

Uniquely, *Whispering City* was shot in French simultaneously with the English version. The Hollywood players, with their Canadian supporting actors, would film the scene in English. Then the Hollywoodians would step from the camera range, and the French-speaking Canadian actors would take over. The French version is known as "La Forteresse". It is no secret to say that the "unknown" French-speaking Canadians outshine the

Hollywood stars, and that the French version is superior to its exciting English counterpart. This augurs well for the future of the Canadian film industry, if these talented players (most of whom are as fluent in English as in French) can be kept in our country. The best will be in all probability lured to Hollywood to join the ranks of Deanna Durbin, Walter Pidgeon, Glenn Ford, Alexander Knox, Alan Young, Raymond Massey, Walter Huston, and other famous transplanted Canadians. This is already the case with Henri Poitras, the extremely convincing police inspector of *Whispering City*, who lowers a smoking revolver with the aplomb of a man engaged in the day's work.

Of more than passing interest in this Canadian film is the part that music plays. The hero is a composer. His "Quebec Concerto" is performed during the film. The actual composition of "Quebec Concerto" is by André Mathieu. André is only seventeen years old, but his Concerto has a maturity and depth far beyond his years. Sympathetically batonned by the noted Canadian conductor, Jean Deslauriers, and played by Canadian musicians, it is a highlight of the film. I will risk predicting that it will have something the same impact as "Warsaw Concerto", when that musical bombshell first exploded upon the films. While the subject matter is not as intense as the latter work, "Quebec Concerto" is brilliant in conception and should have popular appeal. Monsieur Mathieu is now studying in Paris, and he will help build the artistic stature of his native Canada through the years to come.

There are some who will regret that the first Canadian film of importance has to be a melodrama. I will not be amongst those supercilious few. To me, *Whispering City* has moments of Hitchcock suspense against a background to be found nowhere else in the world. If I have any criticism of the picture, it is that there is not enough of the great charm of Quebec City unfolded for our view. The producers can probably argue that their film is entertainment and not a travelogue, but I will reply that *Whispering City* will do more to make tourists want to visit the city in the shadow of Cape Diamond than a thousand travel pictures. No, melodrama was a wise choice. Where an "artistic success" might have killed the infant industry for good and all, this suspense story paves the way for great adventures in the art of the cinema. It is a proving-ground upon which new models can now be tried.

If to my English or American friends I seem to have laid too great stress upon a Canadian achievement that is commonplace in their countries, I can make no apology. Let another country of twelve million citizens (yes, *citizens* at last!) do what Canada has done in the past seven years industrially and artistically, and I will not boast. We now, thanks to my good friends Hugh Maclennan and Gwethalyn Graham, and to Gabrielle Roy whom I have not had the pleasure of meeting, have an international reputation in the field of writing. The National Film Board has been publicizing in Canada magnificently with its cinematic short subjects. Now comes *Whispering City* with its promise of new things in larger fields, and the interest of J. Arthur Rank and other British film producers in things Canadian.

When we have fifty million Canadian citizens, when we are actually as well as in theory one of the greatest countries in the world, such a film as *Whispering City*, such an opportunity as to give you this book, may be of little consequence. Today, these inconsequences have the simple thrill of destiny.

Horace Brown
"Voyageur's Rest,"
Dunbarton, Ontario, June 9, 1947.

16

CHAPTER 1

Quebec is an old and storied city.

When Jacques Cartier first looked in awe at towering Cape Diamond, it was the site of an Indian town, Stadacona. Three-quarters of a century later, Samuel de Champlain founded there the French colony of Quebec. It was on its Plains of Abraham in 1759 that Wolfe and Montcalm met in the battle that was to mean their deaths and was to seal the fate of the whole continent, for here France lost her bid for a Western empire.

Yet Quebec City has remained a bastion of French culture in the New World that the fleur de lys did so much to bring to birth. Here in Quebec City, in its walled Citadel, the last fortified city in North America makes mellow compromise with the past, as it enjoys the present and looks to the future. Here the old and the new meet in respect, each cleaving to each in the city's Upper and Lower Towns– Upper Town with its windswept esplanades, its monumental Chateau Frontenac, its historic walls and battlements, seeming to speak of spaciousness and freedom; Lower Town with its narrow, picturesque streets, its bustling commerce, and its friendly welcome– city of two races, where Roosevelt and Churchill conferred for the sake of Mankind, city where tongue and custom have the flavor of the past, city where a North American antiquity is established and revered, city whose Cape Diamond speaks as a Gibraltar of the North, city that whispers ten thousand times ten thousand tales of past and present– Quebec.

This, then, is a story the city whispers today.

Mary Roberts glanced at the clock. Ten minutes to deadline. The city room of *L'Information* was clothed in its habitual quiet. She lit a cigarette and leaned back idly in her chair. In ten minutes, she would be free to go home to her lonely apartment—

The girl shook the thoughts from her smooth, dark head. She smiled in self-mockery. At twenty-five, financially independent, yet in love with her work and nothing else, she could afford to be tolerant of herself. Perhaps life had been fuller in New York, but she had her doubts. She had been glad of her training in Gotham, but gladder to find a chance to use it in Quebec. Somehow, the charm of the old city had captured her. Even the leisurely pace of *L'Information*, so different from the New York tabloid for which she had written features, was like old wine after a diet of raw gin.

Mary shrugged at her awkward simile. A smile crinkled at the corners of her mouth, a mouth perhaps a little overlarge but skilfully made attractive with just the right amount and shade of lipstick. The smile found its way to her warm, brown eyes.

The hand reaching for the handle of the folding typewriter desk to bring an end to her office day was detoured by the ringing of her telephone. Mary's eyes went automatically to the clock; four minutes to press.

"Rewrite," she said into the mouthpiece.

As the first words jangled through the receiver, she reached for a scratch-pad and began to write, repeating what she had just heard.

"Hotel Dieu ... accident, 5.20 p.m.," she said. "Renée Brancourt ... injured, corner of Dupuis and LaSalle ... right ... resides on Sous le Cap street ... aged 48 ... condition critical ... hit by truck ... I have it! Okay, Georges! Just time to make the last edition! Thanks!"

In thirty seconds, Mary had rattled off a stick, written her own heading, and sent the paragraph on its way to the composing room, where the great presses awaited their daily digest. All in the day's work...

But was it? As she closed her desk, her high forehead puckered in a thoughtful frown.

"Renée Brancourt," she repeated softly. "Now why does that name keep rattling around in my mind? I've heard it somewhere. Maybe Monsieur Durant would know. He knows everything and everybody."

She got up, not very tall, and walked on good legs to a door marked "M. Durant, Redacteur." Her grey tweed suit set off her trim figure. Her very carriage seemed to radiate vitality and poise. Two or three pairs of eyes raised to follow her wistfully, then bent back to their tasks. The owners of those eyes had learnt that Mary Roberts was not interested in just any man, a shock to their various vanities.

"Hullo!" said M. Durant, who hid great brain-power under a mild manner and a bushy, unrevealing moustache. He pushed his glasses back onto his forehead in characteristic gesture. "I was just thinking of you."

"No, thanks," Mary Roberts said promptly.

"My dear young lady!" The famous editor laughed ruefully. "When a man reaches my age and my supposed discretion, and is turned down once by a so charming young lady when he invites her to dinner, he does not repeat his invitation. No, my dear, I was thinking of you in connection with your work."

The woman reporter raised enquiring, well-arched eyebrows, but said nothing.

"You have done well, excellently well! I feared at first that your–ah–hectic experience in New York might have made our little affairs seem paltry. But I find that such is not the case. I am particularly pleased with your coverage of police news, and I have decided to assign you permanently to that beat."

It was what Mary Roberts had wanted for many

months. She hid her delight as well as she could under laconic thanks.

"It will mean an–ah–slight raise in salary," smiled the editor. "Very slight, I might say. I have also decided that I want features from you. I have noticed your interest in Quebec, in its history and in its peoples. Bear that in mind, will you?" The girl nodded, too happy for speech, and he continued kindly. "Now, what was it you wanted to see me about?"

Mary silently handed over her notes. M. Durant looked at them placidly, then his interest quickened.

"Renée Brancourt," he murmured dreamily. "Renée Brancourt. Ah yes! In my day, a name to conjure with … of course, I was very young at the time, you understand."

"Of course!"

"Don't mock me, young lady!" His grin belied his words. "Sometimes I think you are part witch; at other times I know it. Renée Brancourt was a famous actress, when I was young. I remember I had her picture hung in my room."

"Pin-up girl, eh?"

"Something of the sort. But she dropped out of sight, while at the height of her fame with the Comedie Francaise. She was engaged to a wealthy young Quebecker. Let me think–ah yes, his name was, if I am not mistaken in my memory, Robert Marchand. You can check that with our files.

"Yes, sir."

Durant looked fondly at the glossy, bent head, as the girl made busy notes.

"Some day," he said, "you are going to forget business, and then you will make some man *very* happy."

"Why did Renée Brancourt drop out of sight?" came the efficient young voice rather coldly.

The editor sighed. It was a shame to waste so much beauty by giving it talent.

"She did not exactly drop out of sight. Soon after her arrival in Quebec, her fiancé was killed in a fall from Montmorency Falls. The sight deranged the poor woman's mind. She even made fantastic accusations against her fiancé's best friend, the well known Quebec lawyer, Albert Frederick, claiming Albert had pushed Roberts from the cliff. Absurd, or course! I have known Albert Frederick for many years. A fine man and a good citizen."

"Then Renée Brancourt has been in an institution?"

"More than one, I believe. She was released some years ago as cured. I have heard nothing further of her until now." He shrugged his shoulders Gallically. "Eh bien, those you know are as much fodder to the morrow's newspaper as those you don't know. There should be a good feature story on poor Renée Brancourt. Follow it up."

The girl reporter nodded, picked up her notes, and left the office. She went to the newspaper's morgue on the second floor. Jules Laberge, the wrinkled attendant, was locking up for the night, but Mlle. Roberts was a favourite of his, and he said, with a false-toothed smile, that he would be glad to wait five minutes for her.

Under the Bs, Marie found "BRANCOURT, Renée." It was a fairly complete file. She put it in her handbag for further reference along with a picture of a beautiful young woman dressed in the style of twenty years ago. This had been Renée Brancourt at the top of her fame.

On her way out, Mary slipped a protesting Jules Laberge a "pourboire."

"Don't spend it all in one place," she laughed and gave one withered cheek a kiss that left it tingling, and its owner remembering things he had thought forgotten.

At the Hotel Dieu, the girl from *L'Information* was directed to the Charity Ward. There, the Sister in charge, while insisting it was highly irregular, allowed

Mary Roberts five minutes with Renée Brancourt. It was a serious case, but *L'Information* had been kind to the hospital in the past, and one could overlook in this instance …

The starched robes rustled down the echoing corridor, while Mary Roberts followed briskly. She never felt at ease in a hospital, but a reporter cannot have likes and dislikes.

Mary Roberts bent over the bed in a sudden pity. The woman who lay there was a gray-haired, wasted caricature of the beautiful creature in the photograph she had taken from her purse. The years had been unkind to the once-famous actress, but it was more than premature aging that caused the haunted look in the pale eyes the woman turned to her visitor. There was suffering there, and a nameless fear and a hint of a horror lived with and never denied.

"Who is it?" asked Renée Brancourt, her voice near exhaustion.

"It is a young lady from a newspaper," said the Sister softly. "Do you wish to speak with her?"

The tortured head lifted with an effort to give the eyes a full look at Mary. Then the head sank back. The ex-actress gave a brave and pitiful smile, and there were memories in her eyes as they seemed to light from inner fires.

"Ah, the newspapers!" she whispered. "I am glad they've not forgotten me entirely."

The Sister rustled away discreetly. Mary leaned over the bed. What was it like, she wondered, to lie in a bed in a charity hospital, when once the world has been at one's feet?

"The famous are never forgotten, Mlle. Brancourt," she said.

"No?" A bitter edge came on the voice of the injured woman. "Then why am I here, and not in a

24

private ward, surrounded by flowers? I'll tell you why! It is because someone else enjoys what would have been Robert's and mine."

The voice, which had risen almost to a shriek, so that Mary had expected the Sister's return, died away to a broken whisper on the last words. The thin body under the bedclothes was shaken by sobs all the more terrible because the eyes remained dry and hot.

"Robert... Robert..." said Renée Brancourt, as though she spoke to someone who had listened to her for years while not replying. "It will not be for long, my love."

Mary felt as though she had opened a bundle of old love-letters by mistake. Her dark face flushed. She was unaccountably shaken by this woman who lived in the past.

"You speak of Robert Marchand?" the reporter asked. The man who was killed in the accident at Montmorency Falls?"

"Accident!" By a superhuman exertion, Renée Brancourt forced herself erect in the narrow cot. "It was no accident! Robert was killed."

Mary tried to push the woman gently back onto the pillow, but Renée would have none of it. "It wasn't an accident," Renée finally repeated dully, and lay back exhausted.

"But surely –" Mary gestured helplessly. "There was an inquest. The verdict was accidental death."

"He was murdered!" The shriek came back into the poor creature's voice. "I told them, but they laughed at me. He was too strong, too respectable. They said I was insane. They put me away. Ugh! The things I saw then would make anyone crazy. After many years, they said I was harmless. They let me out. Since I was released, I have lived in fear, dreadful fear. Do you know what it is like to be afraid of every shadow?"

25

Mary backed away warily, shaking her head. Surely the poor woman was mad. And yet there was something so sane about her, so appealing and demanding at one and the same time. What was it she had heard about the insane? That they gave great appearance of sanity, except when their particular mania was at its height.

"No, don't go!" the woman pleaded. "You must believe me! I have so little time in which to have my revenge for the sake of poor Robert. Will you make me a promise?" A scrawny hand clutched at the girl, grasped her unwilling arm. "Is it too much for a dying woman to ask of you?"

"You will get well."

"I do not want to get well. I want to do what I could not do for twenty years, die and go to my Robert." The voice was shrilling again, and Mary heard the rustle of starched skirts in the corridor. "Make me a promise before God that you will investigate!"

"Investigate?"

"That you will try to learn the truth."

Almost involuntarily, Mary nodded. The woman sighed with satisfaction.

"It is done," the woman whispered. "It is done, Robert."

Mary Roberts felt a crawling in her flesh, as though she had slept on an ant-hill. It was eerie to think that this poor woman, once the gayest name in Montreal and Paris and an actress of the greatest merit, should have cherished through a score of years these weird notions. And to what had she, Mary Roberts, to whom a promise, was a promise, committed herself? To investigate. To follow a will-o'-the-wisp into nothing.

"I am sorry," said the Sister at the elbow, "but your coming has excited the patient. I must ask you to leave."

"Only another minute, please."

The Sister shook her cowled head, looking with

compassion upon the ghost of the woman who has led a life beyond her devout conception and was now brought to such misery. Mary, seeing Renée Brancourt fight for breath, regretfully understood. Yet her reporter's instinct told her there was still much of the story she should know. Behind all the ramblings of the supposedly demented woman, she sensed a coherent mystery, a mystery she was now pledged to investigate, and, if at all possible, solve.

"Perhaps I could return tomorrow, Sister," she suggested hopefully.

Looking at her critically-injured patient, the Sister answered gently, "If it be the will of God..."

CHAPTER 2

Monsieur Durant rattled the sheets of copy reluctantly.

"An interesting story," he hemmed, "but I am afraid it is more in the New York tradition. On *L'Information* we are inclined to be a little more staid. Our libel laws, you understand, are more strict."

"If you weren't my boss," said Mary Roberts unsmiling, "I'd be inclined to say, 'get to the point.'"

The little editor bowed politely.

"I accept the implied rebuke, Mlle. Roberts. The point is very simple: we cannot publish an article in which a woman once declared legally insane, repeats her accusation of insanity."

"I name no names."

"Memories are long. And yet, for old times' sake, I am interested in a story dealing with Renée Brancourt, a *factual* story, you understand, one that can be published." Durant puffed strongly on a cigarette. "Do I make myself plain?"

Mary shrugged off her disappointment.

"You're the boss," she answered somewhat flippantly.

"I would like a feature on the stage of her day... the plays, the people, the atmosphere. What was the Quebec she knew like?"

The girl's skirt crept up over her nylon-clad knees. She pulled it down again absent-mindedly, and M. Durant looked elsewhere.

"I have a feeling I've talked to the poor woman all I can," she said. "I'll have to get the story somewhere else."

"Then I'll send you to see Albert Frederick."

The editor must have seen the doubt in his reporter's eyes for he hastened on, "I know, I know. He is the man la Brancourt accuses of murdering her fiancé. I think you should meet Albert, if only to realize the absurdity of the charge. Why, I believe he was half in love with Renée himself, and he certainly had a great affection for the unfortunate Robert Marchand, who was his client as well as his friend. Albert is one of the most influential men in Quebec, polished, suave, altogether a man of the world."

Mary made a little moue.

"Oh, *that* kind!"

"You must have had a bad experience with some man," Durant chuckled, "to be suspicious of all men. No, my dear, Albert is the soul of discretion with women. Sometimes I think the man has not the passion to love anything but the Arts. He has helped more struggling artists and authors and musicians through rough paths than any other man I know. He has made proper use of his wealth, I can tell you."

"So, this paragon is also wealthy."

Durant pushed back his spectacles impatiently.

"Please! You must not be cynical. There is a fine story here, if you but follow it through. And Albert can be of help to you on your new police beat. He has great influence with les gendarmes."

Mary threw back her head in a shout of laughter. Then she came around the desk and rumpled the editor's sparse hair.

"You old fraud!" she said. "So, you had that in the back of your mind all the time, when I thought you were only sending me off on a wild-goose chase. How do I get in to see this Albert Frederick?"

"That is very simple." The editor scribbled on a chit. "Give this to the butler. Good luck, little one."

The girl accepted the note, settled her tam more firmly on her head. She looked at herself in the mirror and seemed satisfied.

"Now you are ready for the warpath." The genial editor held up his hands in pretended horror. "What chance has a poor man in this world of women?"

Mary made a face at him, and went out, thinking how kind and quiet M. Durant was, and yet how deeply he thought and how unexpectedly his humor streaked through his pattern of reserve. She wished she could return his kindness with a little feminine interest she knew he would appreciate, yet it was not in her to encourage any man without reason.

The house was on Grande Allee, an imposing three-story edifice in the style of the century. Mary Roberts had been in similar homes in Quebec City. She knew that she would find it hiding its wealth under taste, rather gloomy in its appointments perhaps but with a flair for oil painting and for richly-subdued, if heavy, furniture. Mary preferred her own small but bright and modern apartment high above the city, looking out over the wide St. Lawrence and laying Quebec at her feet. She could not help wondering how one man could enjoy himself living in such lonely grandeur as must exist within this fortress of a house.

An unobtrusive butler answered her ring, and she handed him the note from M. Durant. The butler took it; his manner underwent a subtle change, as he realized he was dealing with a mere reporter, although a pretty one for a change.

"Monsieur Frederick is engaged," he said loftily. "However, if you care to wait, I will present this … ah … document to him.

"That's okay," said Mary easily, from long experience with taking butlers down a peg or two. "You go right ahead and do that little thing. I have all the time in the world."

The butler's back was very straight and stiff. Mary watched it with secret amusement. She was also intrigued by the fact that her guess as to the inside furnishing of the ornate home had been correct. If anything, she had erred on the side of cheerfulness; the Frederick mansion was what Mary's New York friends would have called a "gloomy hole."

When the butler unobtrusively entered the library, he found his employer listening with young Michel Lacoste to a recording of one of the latter's most recent compositions. The servant knew better than to intrude upon such a moment. He silently placed the silver salver before Albert Frederick, who took the note, glanced at it absently, and went on listening.

The wealthy lawyer and patron of the arts gave the impression of power under leash. He was of average height, but he seemed tall and dominating, perhaps because he held himself with such correct straightness. There was an easy strength to his movements, a sense of aristocracy of position that seemed to go with the surroundings. His face was handsome in a still, grey way, and there was almost a military appearance in his grey-sprinkled moustache. Something in the eyes was haunted, but they were a steel-grey, which constant appearances in court had sharpened to a point of half-humorous mercilessness.

His guest, the rising composer Michel Lacoste, was a dark, intense young man with burning eyes and constantly expressive hands that were now moving in time to the music pouring from the radio-phonograph. He had the build and quickness of a boxer, and his full and mobile mouth betrayed his agitation.

The butler stood, and M. Frederick said finally, "Ask her to wait, please."

When they were alone again, Michel Lacoste shook his head. He came to a sudden artist's decision, strode

31

over to the machine and turned off the recording. His face was a mask of despair.

"What did I tell you, Albert?" he demanded. "It's no good! No good at all!"

The lawyer laughed shortly and crossed to the liquor cabinet. He took his time over selecting a bottle.

"You are overwrought, my friend. I thought it a delightful motif, one well worthy of you. It should be finished."

"I cannot finish it," said Michel tragically. "I'm afraid I lack the inspiration. At least it was generous of you to have had it recorded."

"I can afford to be generous where I think talent exists, as it does exist with you. Drink?"

Michel waved acceptance. He watched his host measure out the golden liquid with studied carelessness.

Frederick said, "You artists are never satisfied with yourselves. I tell you, mon ami, you should feel yourself at the moment on top of the world. Your concerto is a great piece of music. I am supposed to have some taste, and I assure you of that. Then, too, you are certain of its performance and–"

"Through your kindness! Always through your kindness. Albert, I can never repay you!"

The lawyer smiled, a thin, grey smile.

"You can and you shall. You shall repay me through reaching the top of your profession and by allowing it to be known that I have been your patron. That is the only reward I ask."

"It is so little!"

"It is a great deal … to me. Allow me to be the judge of that, please." He handed Michel the sparkling glass. "Let's drink to your success."

Michel's lips curled in a boyish sneer.

"Success," he pledged insincerely.

The lawyer put down his glass decisively. He came

over and planted himself firmly in front of the young composer. His hand came down with authoritative friendliness on the other's arm.

"Why don't you confide in me?" he demanded. When he received no answer, he made a lawyer's thrust, "It's Blanche, isn't it?"

Taken aback, Michel stared moodily at his drink for a space. Then, he nodded miserably.

"We can't get along, that's all."

"I see." The lawyer stroked his moustache. "In my business, I see much of unhappy marriage. Another man?"

"There is no other man, no other woman." Michel locked his hands in a mental agony. "It's so hard to explain, unless you're married. It's the little things, the trifling things. They've grown until they've become monstrous. Most of all, she's jealous of my work."

"What wife married to a man of talent isn't, if she possesses no talent herself? She must learn to tolerate, to make allowances. Your work is too precious to be lost because of a woman."

Michel downed the rest of his drink in a gulp. It seemed to steady him. He went to the window and stared out into the silent and deserted street. Its emptiness and dullness after rain suited his mood.

"We were so happy when we were first married," he said to no one in particular. "We talked of a little home, of my doing great work. Then she learnt she could not have a baby. It was a blow. When we had to live in a couple of rooms, she lost her taste for housework. She imagines herself ill all the time. Perhaps she *is* ill. She needs medicine to make her sleep. And she nags me to write popular music."

"Your sort does not write popular music," Frederick interrupted.

"That is what I tell her. But she can only see the

33

pennies that are needed. She thinks my work takes me from her. She is possessive. She wants me to be always with her and to neglect my work." Michel turned back to say to this friend with passionate emphasis, "I am an artist, Albert!"

"Of course you are! But are you sure that this sort of thing cannot be patched up? You are probably overwrought and imagining a great deal."

"You think so, eh? Would you listen to another record, not a musical record, one of different sort?"

Albert Frederick nodded in an obvious effort to humor his excited guest. Michel went to the album he had brought with him and extracted a twelve-inch blank only partially-used.

"I found this in the album this morning," he said. "I wondered what it was doing there. I soon learned when I played it over. Listen!"

He placed the record on the turntable and started the machine. A woman's voice came through the loud-speaker hysterically. It said:

"To whom it may concern: I, Blanche Lacoste, living in constant fear of death with which my husband threatens me, want it known that should I be found dead it was his doing."

That was all. Michel stopped the machine. Albert Frederick looked anywhere but at his friend who had so suddenly been stripped naked before him.

"This sort of thing is not normal," the lawyer said embarrassedly. "You must not pay too much attention to it."

"It's ruining my life! Driving me out of my mind!"

"Yes, I can see it could easily have that effect. Well, there's nothing for it. The concert is the most important event in your life. Try to muddle along until after it is over. On the strength of this record, we should be able to force a separation. Leave it with me."

.Some hope came into Michel Lacoste's face.

"You can't go on like this," Albert Frederick continued with efficient sympathy. "I know. I've seen too many cases of this kind. Today, you're sorry for her. You've made a mistake, but you don't like to let her down. But one day it'll be too much. One day you *will* hate her. She's driving you to a crisis. However, you must return to her, now. Do not give her another excuse for a silly quarrel that upsets you. Besides, I have someone waiting to see me."

"I *have* been a damn fool, haven't I?"

"No, my friend, you have been young. And who would not want to be young in Quebec?" The older man gave the youth a pat on the shoulder. "In case you can't find peace at your home, I can always put you up."

Through sudden, blind tears, Lacoste groped for the lawyer's hand.

"Why are you so good to me, Albert?"

"You know why. It's because I know one day you'll be a very famous man and I want to be mentioned in your biography. You see how vain I am, Michel? You may leave by the side door, if you wish."

The lawyer stood in thought for some moments after his friend had left. Then, as though thinking was bitter, he shook himself.

"It has been worth it," he said to the empty room.

It was as if he convinced himself of something for the ten thousandth time.

CHAPTER 3

In the gloomy foyer, Mary Roberts was becoming restless. She had decided that she much preferred the modern French school of art to the romantic, and that M. Frederick might be a patron of the arts but he could show a little more progress in his views on painting, when the gentleman in question came forward with outstretched hands. He moved soundlessly across the thick-piled carpet, so that he was almost on top of her before she sensed his presence. She gave a little scream and he laughed apologetically.

"Forgive me," he said with a brisk charm, "I did not mean to startle you, Mlle. Roberts. You are from *L'Information*? From my old friend Durant?"

The reporter nodded.

"Then you are most welcome." He followed the line of her gaze to the buxom court beauty of the days of Louis XV. "I see you like the romantic school."

Mary decided to be honest.

"Not particularly," she said.

Where she had expected frigidity, there was instead a sudden thawing. Albert Frederick smiled, a sincere smile that changed his whole face. Behind the legal mask, he stood revealed as one almost boyishly eager to be understood where his artistic taste was in question.

"This is but for show." He waved a dismissing hand about the entire foyer. "I keep it because it is expected of me by all the 'art lovers' who do not understand the first thing about art. But for those like yourself who are initiate, I say, come into my library."

"Said the spider to the fly?"

"Now you are making me feel not only debonair but wicked, mademoiselle. You are a tonic, and I must thank my friend Durant for sending you. Come!" As one used to being obeyed, he turned and led the way through the library door. He waved a designedly negligent hand around the cozy room, where in the fireplace a fire burned cheerfully. "As you will see, I keep the good things always by me … Picasso, at his earliest, and I think best. Van Gogh … when he was enchanted by the mistral of Arles, poor man. Gauguin … striking fire onto canvas from the languid tropics, which he understood as have few white men."

As her involuntary host spoke, Mary Roberts made a tour of the room. She knew it was expected of her, but she was fascinated nonetheless. Her New York Saturday afternoons had often been spent in the Metropolitan Museum of Art. In this private collection there was something much more warm and intimate; she realized of a sudden it was a reflection of her host's personality.

"There is even a Corot or two," he apologized smilingly. "I confess to a fondness for Corot."

"So do I. Especially his smaller canvases, such as you possess."

"Then I shall show you something I reserve only for my guests of honour," Frederick said gallantly. He pulled drawstrings on an alcove. "Voila!"

Mary Roberts held her breath. She did not speak for several moments, and it was the right thing.

"Kreighoff," she whispered finally. "And Tom Thomson! Here is an A.Y. Jackson surely?"

"You are right."

"Even an Arthur Heming. Sometimes I think he is a great artist, sometimes not."

"He baffles, does he not?" The connoisseur was

obviously enjoying himself. "Do you like Franz Johnston? Personally, I find him a trifle photographic."

The girl turned away reluctantly.

"It's so beautiful, Monsieur Frederick, I could have spent hours just adoring it, especially the Canadian artists in this alcove, but I'm afraid I have work to do."

"Ah, work!" The lawyer gave a mock sigh. "It plagues our existence, does it not? Tiens! Will you do me the honour to seat yourself and tell me what it is you wish? I must pay a call on my friend Durant soon. We have lost sight of one another lately, but we have been good friends for more years than I care to remember."

Mary Roberts seated herself in an easy-chair. Her skirt sculpted her thighs.

She said archly, "Surely you're a good deal younger than Mr. Durant?"

"In spirit, at least," he answered, pleased, and she knew his vanity from that first moment. To hide her confusion, she fumbled for a cigarette, but he was ahead of her, offering her ovals from a silver case. "May I? A special blend of Egyptian I have made up for myself. You may find it intriguing."

As he held the light for her, she happened to look straight into his hard eyes. Under their crust she sensed hunger and yearning, coupled with a strange sexlessness. It was as though he found her beautiful, as he found a painting beautiful, not to want in a man's way but to look at and fondle in imagination. The feeling, inexplicable as it was, made her shudder. She took refuge in a strong, fragrant puff, but he had marked her shivering and misunderstood, it might be deliberately.

"You are cold," he said. "Perhaps some brandy?"

"I'd be delighted." She laughed to cover her confusion. "But work, remember? We go to press at midnight."

Albert Frederick brought a dark bottle from the liquor cabinet. He felt himself strangely warmed and stirred by this girl. Durant was a sly one, to employ such as her ...

Ignoring the protest of her hand, he poured reverently from the bottle.

"My dear Mlle. Roberts, it has taken this brandy sixty-eight years to reach its full flavor. I am certain you can spare it five minutes."

Mary joined in his laughter at her expense.

"If you insist–" She watched the golden liquid. "Please, not too much. You see, I'm very anxious to get all the information I can on Renée Brancourt–"

Was it her imagination, or did the hand holding the bottle waver for a moment? No, it must have been a trick of the mind, for the hand was pouring as steadily as ever.

She went on, "And since you knew her and Robert Marchand so well–"

Lawyer Frederick turned towards the girl, holding a tiny glass in either hand. His face was composed and still.

"Renée Brancourt?" he asked, seeming to search his memory. Yet the girl knew instinctively that the name was one that was always with him.

"The one-time actress. I was led to believe you knew her well. There was an accident this evening. She was taken to the Hotel Dieu."

"The hospital?" he whispered.

"Yes. She was hit by a car. I don't think she's expected to live."

Completely master of himself, Frederick extended the small glass of brandy courteously. She sipped. It was fire and velvet at one and the same time, a luxury of the wealthy. When she looked up again, her host had seated himself behind his desk. He had assumed a look of controlled sympathy.

"Poor Renée Brancourt," he said firmly. "She was *so* beautiful. It is unbelievable to what depths a woman can fall! A tragic end to a tragic career." When Mary did not help him out, he took a sip of the brandy, stared for a moment at the fire, and went on, "You bring back sad memories, Mlle. Roberts. She was to be married to my dearest friend. He died in an accident."

"I know." Mary's brown eyes were innocent. "She told me. Only she said—"

The lawyer's white hand closed spasmodically over the glass. It took him an appreciable space of time to recover, yet he was able to interrupt in a carefully controlled voice, "Told you? Then... you have talked with her?"

There was no blood in his face. He leaned upon the desk, as upon her answer.

"Oh, just for a few minutes," the reporter answered, appearing not to notice the reaction her information had created. "I'm to see her tomorrow. Perhaps I should not say this, but the poor soul does not believe Marchand's death to have been an accident. In fact, the opposite."

"Ah yes, I know poor Renée's fixation ... only too well!" The eminent lawyer drew a deep breath. As he spoke, he picked up a packet of paper-matches from the desk, extracted one, and it seemed with the volition of his will, made a most peculiar "doodle" that had some of the aspects of a man drawn with straight lines. "It was most distressing to me when he became engaged to Renée. Robert had not taken my advice and made a new will. To the young, there is always so much time. His old will had left everything to me, to be administered as I saw fit. Naturally, under Quebec law—" He shrugged away the distasteful memory. "I insisted upon the fullest investigation. Renée acted disgracefully at the inquest. There was nothing I could do for the poor girl, particularly in view of the absurd accusations—"

Mary Roberts snuggled like a sleeping cat in the chair. The aged brandy had given her a sense of well-being. In this room of culture and charm, face-to-face with this man who held so high a position, the vague accusations from that forgotten bed in the charity ward of Hotel Dieu seemed, to say the least, fantastic.

"Of course!" She gave the lawyer her best smile. "I am sorry to have been the cause of any trouble to you. But as a reporter – I take it you agree, Monsieur Frederick – that the shock unbalanced Renée's mind?"

The man laid aside the strange doodle and regarded her fixedly.

"My dear," he said with an obvious effort. "I'm not an expert. But two of our leading doctors agreed that it had. There was nothing to do but accept their opinions. They claimed the poor woman had been drinking heavily, and that her mind had never been too strong at the best. There is no doubt she was deeply in love with Robert. Well–"

He spread his hands to end the painful interview. Mary stood up.

"You're right, of course," she said. "But the woman sounded so convincing. You'll forgive me, I–"

"You almost believed her." Frederick laughed harshly. "So did a hard-hearted jury. If it had not been for the testimony of the alienists– Eh bien, one must not have hard feelings at a time like this. I will call the hospital. If there is anything money can do for poor Renée–"

There was such a ring of sincerity in the man's voice that Mary felt ashamed of her previous vague suspicions. After all, it had happened twenty years ago, and surely if there was justice anywhere and a crime had been committed something would have come to light in all that time. How could she have taken the word of an admittedly insane woman against the record of this great criminal lawyer?

"I've upset you; I'm sorry," she said contritely, settling her tam in characteristic gesture on her smooth head. "It was just that Monsieur Durant thought you might be able to give me some personal details for a human-interest story."

Frederick smiled wanly and came around the desk to her. She could find it in her heart to pity him, his loneliness, his solitary grandeur, living in a dream world of Art of his own where only a few could penetrate and where she had been for a few moments a privileged visitor.

"I *am* upset," the great man confessed. "This comes as rather a severe shock. I would like to tell you a story as a last service to Renée. She was like a child with candy about publicity. But I'm afraid I'm not really up to it just now. Suppose I call Durant in a couple of days. Then if you don't mind coming back–"

"Mary looked around the cozy room.

"I'll be glad to. Perhaps you might even let me look in the alcove again? At any rate, thanks for all your kindness to me."

The lawyer followed her to the library door with old world courtliness, ushered her through to the street door. The air was fresh and crisp after the rain. She suddenly realized how stuffy the old home had been.

"At least I've had the good fortune to make your acquaintance," Frederick said, but the girl knew with her man experience that the words were mechanical and that his thoughts were far away, perhaps twenty years far away.

They shook hands politely, but she did not hear the door close behind her. At the corner, she turned. Albert Frederick was still watching her. When he saw her pivot, he closed the door hastily.

"A strange, inquiring man," she told the night and felt something long dormant stir within her.

Back in the library, Albert Frederick sat in the flickering shadows of the wood fire and thought. It had been so carefully buried these twenty years, and now there were footsteps on the grave.

He poured himself a stiff drink of the mellow brandy. His hand was unsteady, and the rims of the bottle and glass rattled together musically. The drink was tossed off as though it were water. In the fireplace, his face was mephistophelean. The lines in his face deepened. He aged years in seconds.

"Not to sleep," he murmured. "Not to sleep... again."

The room closed in about him. Its shadows seemed to whisper and reach, as the city had whispered and reached for so long a time. He had earned peace; he deserved peace.

Making a decision, he went back to the desk and lifted the receiver from the telephone. As he did so, the actor in the lawyer came to the surface, wiping out the lines. He dialed the number of the hospital with a sure finger.

"Hotel Dieu?" he enquired. "I am calling to enquire the condition of Mlle. Brancourt. No, not a relative, merely an old friend. I see … I see … A half-hour ago? Yes, it is very sad. Thank you. Thank you very much."

Albert Frederick replaced the receiver.

"Dead," he whispered, and in his voice was a new lightness and desire for living. "Poor Renée. I must see she gets a decent burial."

It was a habit to talk to himself aloud. It gave his lonely life at least one voice.

Lighting a cigarette, the lawyer pondered something deeply, apparently giving the thought as much care as he would have given an intricate case for a client. Then he reached for the telephone directory, quickly found the number of *L'Information*, dialed.

"Hullo, Monsieur Durant, please." His long fingers drummed the desk-top while he waited. "Monsieur Durant? Edward, this is Albert, Albert Frederick. Yes, it has been a long time, hasn't it? We must make amends for that at luncheon some day soon. Edward, I want to congratulate you upon your taste in reporters. Très chic! You old rascal!" He grinned nervously as words rattled back at him. The fireplace gave his face a ruddy, unnatural glow. "You think of her only as a reporter, eh? It is as a reporter I am thinking of her as well. Old friend, why assign a reporter, even one so charming, to reopen old wounds? Poor Robert is dead these twenty years... and now Renée. Yes, I just called the hospital. Not a half-hour ago. Is it not sad? Edward, let their ashes rest in peace. A brief obituary is all that is required. It would please me, and it would be best for Renée and Robert. Thank you, Edward. Bon soir."

He replaced the receiver with a small sigh. Then he began to shake with racking sobs.

In that small, empty room, it was a horrible performance without visible audience.

CHAPTER 4

When Mary Roberts came into the drab atmosphere of *L'Information*, it was like a breath of fresh Quebec air. Her cheeks were glowing from her walk in the magic of the night. She had been intoxicated anew by the mystery and charm of this city she called her own, and if Monsieur Frederick's excellent brandy had been any assistance it was only to lend an extra sparkle to the exciting eyes.

Monsieur Durant did not look up, when she sauntered into his office. Mary knew what that meant. Like a boy caught stealing apples from the neighbour's orchard, the editor could not face anyone when he had unpleasant news to impart or when he had done something that troubled his editorial conscience.

"Your friend is very nice," Mary said.

"I was just talking to him on the telephone." Durant went on correcting copy, his practiced pencil fairly flying. "He told me that Renée Brancourt died a half-hour ago."

The reporter felt as though she had been slapped. Somehow, of all the tragedies she had encountered in the past four months, the one that had taken the firmest hold on her imagination was that of this day.

"Oh! The poor woman!" she said with quick sympathy. "Monsieur Frederick must have telephoned the hospital directly after I left."

"So?"

"Nothing." The reporter looked thoughtfully at the incipient bald spot on the bent head. "A very refined man, your friend."

45

The editor looked up at last. He laid his pencil aside and pushed his spectacles up on his forehead.

"What do you mean?" he asked, puzzled.

"What could I mean? His furniture … his liquor … his paintings …"

"Oh yes, of course. Albert is a connoisseur, great believer in beauty. I would say that Beauty is his goddess. There is nobody in Quebec who does more for the Arts. As for charity, nobody is ever turned away by Albert Frederick. A queer mixture in a man, so much gentleness and ruthlessness combined."

Mary lit a cigarette. She looked at Durant over the flame of her match.

"Ruthlessness?"

"You should see him in a courtroom, as you probably will on your new beat. I have seen Albert reduce a confident opposition witness to pulp, and then mash him around for another hour. Eh bien, I am busy."

"The Brancourt story?"

"Treat it as a routine obituary. What is it they say it is best to do with sleeping dogs?"

The girl flicked ashes on the floor and said, "Let them lie. It all depends how you use the verb." She shrugged. "Well, if that's the way Monsieur Frederick wants it—"

Durant pounced on the unfinished sentence.

"What do you mean?" he demanded. "That's how *I* want it!"

"Of course, Monsieur Durant, naturellement." She smiled with a woman's mock respect in a way that boils a man's blood. "You are the editor of this paper, so nothing your friend, Albert Frederick, could say could influence you in the slightest."

The head was down again, but the bald spot had a pink tinge to it. Durant was too good a newspaperman not to feel a shame at being caught at that oldest of journalistic tricks, pleasing the influential. He began to fumble around for his spectacles.

"On your forehead," the girl told him from the doorway.

A groping hand found them. He looked up pleased, wanting her good opinion for some obscure reason.

"How did you know?" he smiled timidly.

"Maybe I'm psychic," she answered with unnecessary emphasis.

Seated at the familiar desk, she pulled off her gloves slowly. There seemed no point to her, now, in typing the story of Renée Brancourt. The feast of writing she had envisioned had turned to a meagre, tasteless repast. Still, it was a job that had to be done.

She was writing "-30-" at the end of the short, stilted obituary, when the seventy-year-old "copy boy" said there was someone who wanted to see her. Mary gave the bald head an affectionate pat and went out into the waiting-room. To her surprise, her visitor was a young girl wearing the uniform of a convent.

"You interviewed Mlle. Brancourt earlier this evening, did you not?" the girl asked.

"Yes …"

"I am sorry to tell you she passed away," the girl said with quiet sympathy.

"I know. I just heard."

"I live at the Hotel Dieu. I am a ward of the nuns. Mlle. Brancourt was conscious until the end; and in considerable pain. She made me promise that I … it was to humor her, you understand … that I would bring you these." The girl laid two keys on a cheap nickel key ring in the girl reporter's hand. "The matter seemed of the greatest importance to her."

Mary turned the keys over and over stupidly.

"Did Mlle. Brancourt say what these keys were for?"

"For her room– 117 Rue Sous le Cap."

47

"117 Sous le Cap?"

"Yes. She said you were to search her room. There was apparently a diary–"

"I see," said Mary, although she did not. "Thank you very much for your trouble."

"I was pleased to do it," answered the young girl softly. "She was always so nice to me. She had a hard life that one. I trust she has found peace at last."

The girl bowed her way out with dignity, her simple duty done. Mary Roberts continued to twirl the keys in her fingers. Then she looked at her watch. It was almost eleven-thirty. Hardly a time to be visiting a street like Sous le Cap alone, but her nose for news was twitching.

She went back to her desk and slipped out the little .32 automatic she had a police permit to carry. When it was in her handbag she was comforted. She signed out in the assignment book.

Outside, there was a slight fog in Lower Town. It was a chilly, dismal night, and she drew her raincape more closely about her. Even as she asked herself whether she should not wait until morning, she rejected the question. Mary knew that there would be no sleep until she had seen that diary.

A taxi rattled by, and she hailed it, but it went on into the gloom. It was not more than fifteen minutes' walk from the office to Sous le Cap, anyway, so she trudged on.

The smooth pavement gave way to cobblestones. They were greasy with damp. Her steps rang hollowly, as though she walked in a great shaft. The streets narrowed and closed in around her brazenly. She seemed to be walking up and down steep hills to which there were no beginnings and no ends. The city whispered, where before she had found them friendly.

Under a dim, fly-specked light, Mary Roberts found a sign that said "Rue Sous le Cap." She went up the narrow, twisting street, conscious of its reputation, starting at its shadows. The automatic was transferred from her handbag to her suitcoat pocket. Its coldness gave her warmth. Once, she thought herself followed. Twice, she looked back, but the street was empty.

The thin, tall houses, leaning decrepitly against one another, shut out all but the meagerest of stars. The night gave the rabbit-warren a certain stealthy dignity. Eyes, she knew, followed her progress up the street.

The numbers were very hard to make out. She took a pencil flashlight from her purse, aware of the danger of showing a light. Human derelicts might wait in one of those dark alley-mouths for her. From one of the windows, where streaks of dirty light showed through, came the raucous laughter and idiotic screams of a drunken woman. But most places were quiet, for these were cheap boarding-houses in the main, last refuges of those against whom the city has whispered, and their occupants slept the sleeps of those who have bent their backs to heavy tasks and now snatch a few hours of snoring peace before the deadly round for small money begins again.

After her heart had stopped beating several times, Mary found "Numéro 115." She almost dived through the next door, into a long dingy corridor, scarcely wide enough for a big man to pass through. A dim light glowed at the end of the corridor. Mildewing wallpaper hung in shreds from the walls. Lath showed through where the plaster had given up the struggle against the damp. It seemed incredible that the butterfly that was Renée Brancourt had had to end out its life in this human dungheap.

Keeping a firm clutch on the butt of her gun, the girl reporter made for the stairs that wound up into the noisome darkness. She began to regret the whole adventure but was too stubborn or too much the newspaperwoman to draw back. Besides, what lay ahead could be scarcely less frightening than what was behind. Determined, she put her foot on the first stair, when a stealthy sound made her turn, her fingers panicky against the trigger.

A hag of a woman, shapeless, hated by and hating Life, glowed at her with reddened eyes from between hanks of dirty grey hair. The woman clutched a mop threateningly but made no move toward the girl.

"Well?" she demanded, the word exploding in the interval between them. "What do you want at this hour?"

"I have come for Mlle. Brancourt."

The woman made a pathetic attempt at an ingratiating smile that only served to show wide stretches of toothless gum marked off by the odd, decayed snag of a tooth. Her eyes were hungrily on Mary's clothes. She scratched herself reflectively, so that Mary itched just watching her.

"She's not home," the woman said sullenly.

"I know." Mary made her voice rapid and very friendly. "She has been injured in an accident and is in the Hotel Dieu. She gave me her keys and asked me to get some things from her room."

Mary dangled the keys, where they could be easily identified but not snatched.

"Yeah," said the woman finally. "I guess it's okay. I gotta go on with my cleanin'. It's the third floor back. Number 7. Watch your step on them stairs. They ain't too safe, if you ain't used to 'em." Her eyes spoke unfathomable jealousies. "We ain't used to your kind around here much."

The girl fled up the stairs, spurred by the eyes that followed her.

A drunken man swayed in the door of a second storey room. He grinned morosely, as he saw the trim, unexpected figure of the girl, made a grab for her. She pushed him in wild disgust, and he fell over and was sick. Mary stepped over him, numb with courage found somehow, and continued on her way. Her high heels made incisive noises on the worn treads.

In Renée Brancourt's wretched room, near the rickety iron bed, a gloved hand reached for the mattress and threw it back.

At that moment, the clack of high heels on the stairs reached the figure by the bed. He stiffened, muttered a curse, cast a look around. The only possible hiding-place was in the kitchen, where the door sagged open showing the dead actress' definite poverty. The man pulled his fedora well down over his eyes. His long, black overcoat blended with the fetid darkness of the unaired room. In three swift strides, he had unscrewed the lone electric light bulb. Two more steps took him within the kitchen. He closed the door, all but a crack. One eye gleamed through this malignantly.

The intruder waited.

Mary Roberts tried one of the keys in the door marked "7." It did not work. She tried the other. It was useless too. Puzzled, she turned the handle. The door swung inwards, revealing a pit of blackness, through which, as her eyes became accustomed to the lack of light, a greyer darkness stood out from the grimed window-panes.

She took a tentative step into the room. A board squeaked somewhere in the room, and she froze. When the sound was not repeated, Mary looked for the light switch. It was beside the door. She clicked it once, twice, without result.

Her pencil torch picked out a candle on the table beside the bed. She took a paper pack of matches from her handbag, but her hands were shaking so badly it took three tries before she could light a match and transfer the flame to the candle.

"I'll have to stop being a goose," she told herself. "After all, there's nothing to be afraid of."

The candle lit the room with an eerie glow, not reaching its farther recesses, creating huge and menacing shadows. The girl saw the turned back mattress and something clutched and squeezed her heart. In this room of a dead woman, fear lurked.

She turned the keys over and over in her hands, wondering. Someone had obviously searched this room. For what? The hag downstairs? Perhaps. And why two keys? Why the open door?

Mary held her flashlight to the door lock. It had been forced, not too expertly. The marks of the instrument were on the varnished metal.

Her fearing eyes roamed the room. They fastened finally on the bottom drawer of the bureau. There must be a reason for the good, stout lock on that drawer. The girl had mentioned a diary.

What else could be of value in that tawdry room? Surely not the pitiful photographs of Renée at the height of her career, or that silver-mounted photograph of the handsome young man with the weak chin, who must have been Robert Marchand. No, it had to be that locked drawer.

A shadow moved in the kitchen. The candle caught and lost the gleam of an eye through the crack of the door.

Mary tried the smaller key in the lock. It turned easily. The drawer squeaked open under her pull. Within was a jumble of old theatrical programs, yellowed reviews, more photographs of Renée in the scenes of her triumphs.

Suddenly, there came a distinct sound from the kitchen. The skin crawled along Mary's neck. She knew for certain, now, that she was not alone in this room on Rue Sous le Cap.

Everything within her cried out to retreat through the door. But an instinct deeper than herself, the training of the reporter, led her to pick up the candle and advance tremblingly towards the kitchen.

Behind the door, the man waited, taking his breath in little, inaudible sips. He did not want to kill her, but if he had to... He flexed his long hands soundlessly.

Mary pushed the door wider. The light glinted on the blue of her gun-barrel. She slipped off the safety-catch. The flame of the candle reached into the kitchen and threw out the shadows. The girl began to laugh in hysterical relief.

"Well, kitty," she said to the hungry cat, looking up at her with unblinking eyes, "you'd better lend me one of your nine lives. You've just frightened me out of one of mine!"

The cat walked out of the kitchen, his tail erect. He rubbed against the girl.

"I'll take care of you, when I'm through here," she promised. "Poor thing! I suppose you've been locked up all day."

The bounce back from fear was so complete that Mary began to hum gaily to herself, as she returned to her task of turning out the drawer. Finally, she gave an exclamation, and fished out a leather-bound book. It bore the legend "Five Year Diary" and was signed "Renée Brancourt." Mary set the candle on the floor and began to turn the pages excitedly by its guttering light.

She was so absorbed, she did not hear the slight creak of the kitchen door. If she had turned, she would have seen a black-clad figure stealing towards her, a figure twice as tall as life and with the look of an outraged demon on its mask of a face.

In that incalculable moment of Time, heavy footsteps clumped on the stairs. Mary Roberts gasped, rose to her feet, shoved the diary hurriedly into her handbag. She did not notice the shadow that melted back disappointedly to its lair in the kitchen.

"Well?" asked the cleaning woman suspiciously, unaware of her role of guardian angel.

Mary sighed in relief.

"I–I didn't know what to think when I–I heard you. I–I was just leaving." The reporter edged towards the door. "I can't find what Mlle. Brancourt wants. I'll have to come again tomorrow."

She shoved a dollar bill into the cleaning woman's worn hands and fled. The last echo of her heels died away. The woman looked at the bill.

"It will buy you a moment of forgetfulness," she said aloud, and wheezed away. What happened in Life was no concern of hers.

The man came out of the kitchen, careless now of being seen. He strode to the window. The girl was running down Sous le Cap. He watched bitterly as she disappeared into the shadow of Cap Diamond.

"First round to you, Renée," said Albert Frederick softly, as one used to talking to the dead.

CHAPTER 5

It was noon-hour, when Mary Roberts hurried into Quebec's magnificent "Palais de Justice." Her face was pale and drawn from the excitement of her adventure on Sous le Cap plus lack of sleep while she read through the interesting, sometimes lurid, always informative diary of Renée Brancourt. Now, the girl reporter was coming to confirm certain suspicions that the diary had aroused. In her heart was both a fear and a resolve: a fear of the consequences of what she was undertaking; a resolve to see it through.

As she had read through the night in her lonely apartment on the Hill, the wind moaning in from the St. Lawrence and lending eerie accompaniment to the singular tale of horror and human depravity in the diary, she had been seized with the magnitude and boldness of one, Albert Frederick. If the diary was to be believed (and, even discounting its hysteria and vengefulness, it carried a note of sincere conviction throughout, for what woman troubles to confide untruths to a diary she expects nobody to see but herself?), the noted criminal lawyer was a false friend, a thief, a liar, and a murderer.

Alone in her apartment, the diary had seemed real, as a murder mystery seems real to the hair-raised reader at three in the morning. In the bright light of this sunny Quebec day, she reviewed the past events with less conviction and a slackening of moral courage. It seemed, in looking back, that the only thing real about the nightmare of the night had been the general hospitality of Albert Frederick. How was it possible to conceive of this man who had so much and who lived so graciously and generously as the monster depicted in the diary of an admittedly mad woman? Yet how, too, could one ignore that Renée Brancourt had known she was dying, and had relied upon her, a stranger but from the Press, to bring her the vengeance her poor heart desired, even from beyond the grave?

Mary shrugged her shoulders prettily, and tapped brisky along the marble floor, while masculine heads turned to watch her twinkling legs. Her mission today should resolve many questions for her. As it was her day off, her time was her own. She went with youthful assurance through a door marked "Archives."

An hour later, Mary came out the same door. Her bounce was not quite as pronounced. She walked slowly, and there was a thoughtful air about her, as though she were Pandora and had at last opened the forbidden box.

An all-too familiar voice said pleasantly, "Why, Mlle. Roberts! This *is* a pleasure!"

Mary looked up into Albert Frederick's face. His lips were smiling, but his eyes were cold and watchful and, to her, frightening.

"Oh!" she said, and added inanely, because she was flustered, "I–I was just thinking of … you."

"I'm honored," said the lawyer, bowing slightly.

She thought he looked especially handsome and distinguished in his lawyer's robes. The court had no doubt recessed. Had he found her by accident? Did he know where she had been for the last hour? It was impossible to tell from the mask he wore.

"I was contemplating lunch at the Chateau Frontenac," he said smoothly. "I insist on the pleasure of your company."

It would be rude to refuse. Besides, she might learn much. Mary held out her hands impulsively.

"Thank you, Monsieur Frederick. Give me fifteen

minutes in which to make myself presentable."

"You are that already, mademoiselle," he assured her, "and more. But it shall be as you say. Suppose we meet on the Terrace, then, in that time?"

She smiled and walked on, not daring to look back. The Frotenac was across the street, raising its magnificent pile over the city, symbol of the wealth and the luxury that could rise above the poverty of the masses and ignore the existence of that poverty. In its powder-room she could find those moments she needed in which to compose herself to face this man who had so suddenly become a dangerous antagonist.

Albert Frederick watched the girl, a sardonic smile playing about his thin lips. He touched his moustache vaguely, then turned and walked purposefully along the hall to the door marked, "Archives." When he went into the musty room, he found the gnome of a man, Monsieur Petitpas ("they built the place around him," said the flippant younger generation of legal lights), who had been in charge of the Archives ever since he could remember. M. Petitpas was enjoying the last crumbs of a not-too-expensive lunch. Albert Frederick thought incongruously of the coming meal at the Chateau. It was worth a great many things not to have to eat lunch in an unaired room surrounded by the past.

"What? Must I always find you eating?" he asked with a false joviality.

Petitpas licked his withered fingers reflectively.

"But of course, Monsieur Frederick!" he answered with the familiarity of long service. "A man must live."

Frederick smiled cynically.

"Why, good Petitpas? *Why* must a man live?"

"With me it's become a habit," the aged gnome chuckled. "Something I can get for you, Monsieur?"

"Don't disturb yourself, my friend," the lawyer said quickly, coming around the corner to cut off any suggestion of the attendant rising. "The young lady who was here just now ... "

"Ah yes!" Petitpas winked. "My word, *yes!*"

The lawyer assumed the conspiratorial air Petitpas seemed to expect.

"A friend of mine, you understand, Petitpas. She has mislaid her lipstick. She thought perhaps here. I said I'd look for it."

Petitpas washed down the remains of his lunch with cold tea. He gestured towards the rear of the book-lined room.

"She was over there," he said, with man-to-man understanding. "Third alcove."

Frederick moved off in the direction indicated. Over his shoulder, he said casually, "She certainly managed to get herself dusty."

"No wonder," Petitpas called out. "Nobody's dug in those Marchand files for more years than I can remember!"

Albert Frederick missed a step, but said nothing. His hands were clenched in front of his robe so that the knuckles were white. He stopped at the table where Mary had been working. It was littered with bound books labeled Marchand Inquest: in which newspaper accounts and typed records were pasted.

While he hunted feverishly for some clue to the trend of Mary Roberts' investigation, he spoke aloud for Petitpas' benefit and apparently in some annoyance, "Now where the devil would a woman leave a lipstick? I don't know why it is they're always losing or dropping things?"

His white, well-kept hands moved swiftly but found nothing on the desk. He turned his attention to the wastepaper basket. There he found several crumpled pieces of copy-paper. He discarded the first two, but the third set his face into hard, grim lines and his eyes held a hint of despair.

The note read, in a woman's neat handwriting:

"Check time required drive Quebec to Montmorency Falls and return (Page 126– Diary).

"Frederick executor Marchand estate. See if any records available showing repayment Frederick's $45,000 note dated 4-6-25. (Page 160– Diary)."

There was more, but it had been torn off.

"Clever," the lawyer murmured. "Too clever."

On his way out, Monsieur Petitpas asked, "Did you find that which you were seeking, Monsieur Frederick?"

The slender, artistic fingers caressed the stiff moustache.

"Yes," he said, "I did, thank you. Women are so careless."

Over demitasse, Albert Frederick watched the girl. She was half-turned, looking out breathless over the panorama of Quebec and the harbor as it lay supine at her feet. Beautiful, he thought, in a dark and small way, beautiful and dangerous as only a lovely woman with brains can be dangerous. Yet a woman means nothing to me as such, he reflected, and I can look at her beauty as beauty was looked at by Nicholas Nickleby, "skin stretched over a grinning skull."

The girl tuned back to her escort at last.

"I never tire of gazing at Quebec," she said. "It is the most beautiful city in the world."

"And yet some of it is sordid."

Her dark eyes clouded.

"Is not that the way it is in all life, Monsieur! The façade hides the inner decay."

Mary's face came closer, while he lit her cigarette from the paper pack of matches on the table. Her eyes, he decided, as he made his strange doodle with the burnt-out match from habit, were too candid.

"A queer little thing," she said, indicating the doodle.

He laughed, embarrassed.

"We all have our eccentricities. This is mine. Tell me, have you seen Quebec in Winter? That is when it is really beautiful!"

"No, but I'm looking forward to the snow."

"You ski, do you?"

"No, I prefer the more sedate pleasures of life."

His look burnt her with its intensity, as he added:

"I would warn you, our mountain trails are sometimes very dangerous."

"Yes, so I understand." Mary smiled.

The tips were off the epees.

"I take it then, Mlle. Roberts, that it does not frighten you?"

Mary took a deep puff and blew it out reflectively before she answered.

"One can't very well be a sportsman and a coward at the same time."

The thrust went home. But Frederick was too good a verbal swordsman to leave the opening long unprotected. They were looking at each other, suddenly hating each other.

"I agree with you," he answered the girl, "but a really good sportsman knows his limitations and never takes unnecessary chances, no matter how thrilling the game."

"Really?" Mary raised her eyebrows provocatively.

"It is sweet of you to worry about me... I'll be careful."

CHAPTER 6

The billboard outside Palais Montcalm read:

Thursday, October 15th
at 8:30 p.m.
Jean Deslauriers
and his
Symphony Orchestra
present the
World Premiere
of
Michel Lacoste's
"Quebec Concerto"

Within the empty theatre, cheerless as such a place is when used for rehearsal, the orchestra wound up a morning session in its shirtsleeves. Michel Lacoste listened intently as Conductor Deslauriers led the strings through the third movement. It was obvious the composer's nerves were raw.

"No, no, Jimmy," he called. "Wait!"

Deslauriers tapped with his baton, and the players halted. The bassoon began to discuss with the viola the habits of petunias. Bass yawned; the baby had been restless during the night.

"Would you do that again, a little slower?" said Michel, rubbing his hands together restlessly.

"As you say, Michel," shrugged the conductor. "You're paying the shot, or rather Monsieur Frederick."

"Leave him out of this!"

"I'm sorry, Michel. It's been a long rehearsal."

Michel touched his arm understandingly.

"And I've been trying. You'll have to forgive me, mon ami. It's Blanche. I wish she could leave me alone for at least one rehearsal. Particularly one of this importance. Sometimes I think–"

Deslauriers looked at his old friend quickly and compassionately.

"Think nothing rash, Michel, and you'll do nothing rash. He tapped for the orchestra and raised his voice. "All right, men. Once again. More slowly this time, please."

A telephone shrilled backstage. Moments later an attendant called, "Monsieur Lacoste, c'est Madame."

Michel's face was dark with fury.

"Again!" he muttered. "And still once again. She goes too far."

Deslauriers said to the orchestra resignedly, "Take a break, boys. Five minutes."

The composer grabbed up the receiver. His voice was hoarse with rage. It carried to the embarrassed orchestra.

"Hello!... Blanche, why must you continue to call me? You must stop it, you understand!... I'm not a feeble-minded child. You don't have to remind me five times you want something done... Look! In a quarter-hour, we'll be finished the runthrough. I'll come straight home … Yes! Yes. Yes. I'll stop at the drugstore for your prescription. Now, will you *please* let me go?"

Michel Lacoste slammed the receiver back on the hook with unnecessary force. He saw Deslauriers looking at him.

"Well, what are you staring at?" he snarled. "You've seen a henpecked husband before, haven't you? Get on with the rehearsal!"

Then, for a few blessed minutes, he lost his anger in the flowering musical beauty he had created.

Michel Lacoste paused at the door of his motheaten walkup apartment. The wildest swing music assailed the door panels and won its way through noisily to the hall. His shoulders dropped, as he fitted his key into the lock.

The woman on the chesterfield had once been beautiful in a full-blown blonde way. Now she was frowsy. Although it was late in the day, she had not bothered to dress but wore a soiled negligee.

Cigarette butts littered the floor around her. It was obvious the apartment had not been cleared in some time. Blanche Lacoste's appearance was further matted by a premature look of discontent, as if she had bitten into Life and found it continually bitter. It was hard to see what she and Michel had in common.

When her husband opened the door upon the blare of music, she laid aside the confessions magazine she had been reading or pretending to read.

"Oh, so it's you!" she said sarcastically. "How charming of you to come home!"

Her husband laid his music portfolio on the littered table. He made no attempt to go to her, but seated himself at the piano instead. The petulance around her mouth understandably deepened.

"Is that the best you can do?" she nagged. "Here I've been alone all day, and you come home and sit down at the piano. I don't know whether I can stand it. My head is beginning to ache."

"No wonder with that racket." He had placed the score of his concerto on the music-rack and tried to concentrate on making the corrections needed.

"You'll have to forgive me, I have work to do. With the premiere so close, I need every spare moment."

"Everything is more important than me." Blanche flung the magazine on the floor. "All you think of is work, work, work. Why not of me once in a while?"

Michel made a couple of notations, then turned to her. His ears hurt from the phonograph.

"A man's work is important, too."

"I know. I look years older than I am. I haven't any color."

"Then why don't you get some fresh air and sun? You'll go mad, cooped up in this place day and night."

The woman drew the negligee about her sagging breasts.

"And if I went out," she asked malevolently, "who would I talk to? The lamp-posts?"

Michel made a visible attempt to gather the frayed rags of his temper.

"Why can't you make some friends?"

"I can't be bothered. There are too many stupid people in the world."

With a smothered oath, Michel bounced from the piano-stool and strode to the recorder. He snapped off the playing-arm, and the sudden stoppage of the music seemed to leave a hole in the air.

"Blanche," he said, keeping restraint in his voice by a visible effort, "you'll have to understand. I have work to do, hard work, and I'm very tired."

"You're tired," the woman sneered. "Well, I'm sick."

"I know you're sick." He spoke gently this time, like a person speaks to an unreasonable but loved child. "I wish there were something I could do for you."

"There is!" Blanche stood up for the first time since he had come into the room. She was listlessly tall. "You can love me!"

"I do love you," he answered unconvincingly.

The harshness of her laughter showed she was not misled. The laughter segued into a fit of coughing that shook her whole body and left her gasping. He put a commiserating hand on her heaving shoulder, then went back to the piano helpless.

"The doctor says I need a complete rest," she whined at last, seeking his pity. "He told you anything might happen, if I don't get complete rest."

"I know. I've tried to send you away."

"There! What did I tell you? You'd love to get rid of me, wouldn't you?"

Michel Lacoste flung down his pencil angrily.

"What the hell's a man to do?" he demanded. "I suppose it's the old story. I'm damned if I do, and I'm damned if I don't."

"You want to get rid of me."

He could have cheerfully shaken all the breath out of her.

"I want you to go away for a rest, like the doctor ordered. That's all!"

"You'd do anything to get me out of the way."

Seeing the uselessness of further argument, Michel mumbled something about "having to work," and picked up his pencil again. The woman pounced upon him like a hungry tigress.

"Sure! Sure you have to work!" she screeched. "It doesn't matter if I'm dying, you have to finish your lousy concerto. And for what?" Her sneer was incredible. "For another measly three hundred bucks! Like your blasted symphony last year."

All the blood drained from the composer's face. It seemed he could scarcely support his anger.

"Is that all my work means to you?" he asked, his voice low and trembling. "Money?"

Her hands were claws, as she raked the air in her fury.

"Why don't you get wise to yourself, Michel? You're wasting your time. Why don't you write popular songs, like you did in college? Oh, I know! It isn't Art! Well, to hell with Art! I'm young, and I want to have fun. I want to see something of life. Do you think I'd have married you, if I'd known I was going to spend the best part of my life in this dump?" She was beside herself, when she saw that he had seemingly paid no attention but gone ahead with the changes in the score. "Well, why don't you answer?"

Michel almost saw the humor of the situation.

"There isn't any answer, Blanche," he said, quietly. "Either you love someone or you don't. Love implies belief, belief in a man and belief in his work. You have no faith in me."

If Blanche had had any real tears left in her neurotic system, she would have cried. The words touched her, more than she cared to admit to herself. Her only trouble, she knew, was loving a man who had gone beyond her. She looked at the dark, intense young man, bent it seemed forever over his music, swallowed up in his music, lost to her in his music, and she almost heard the crack in her heart and the pain was blinding. Blanche sank back upon the couch, exhausted. It was not in her, however, to keep still. Womanlike, she wanted more argument.

"Naturally, you forgot my sleep medicine," she said nastily, and had to repeat her assertion before he came partially out of the deep concentration into which he had learned to thrust himself when she began one of her endless quarrels.

"Eh? Oh yes, your medicine. It's in my briefcase."

Blanche went swiftly to the leather case, rummaged in its contents. She found a small box, lifted it out. The directions read: Take one injection at bedtime. AN OVERDOSE MIGHT BE FATAL." Inside were a number of ampoules. She sat down again, holding the box thoughtfully.

Blanche wheedled, "I want to go out to dinner."

"Why don't you?"

"You don't expect me to go alone, do you?" she

66

asked incredulously, turning the box over and over in nervous fingers.

"Look Blanche, surely I can't make it any plainer? I have to make these changes in the score for tomorrow's rehearsal. It's not easy." His tone became more irritable. "Stay in or go out but stop bothering me."

"I can't stand another minute in this pigsty!" his wife blazed.

"Then clean it up," he answered callously.

That tore it again.

"I'm so sick I can hardly see, but you want me to get on my knees and scrub floors!" she spat out. Then a cunning expression came on her unhealthy face. "And I know why, too. Don't think I don't. You hope it will kill me!"

Michel started at this caricature of a wife.

"That's nonsense! Do you know what? I think you enjoy these scenes. They've become like dope to you. You *need* them. Well, I don't Blanche. Someday you're going to drive me a little too far. Someday you're going to say just one thing too many."

"That's right! Go ahead! Threaten me! Kill me, if you want! Kill me, if it'll make you happy!"

Disgusted with himself for having allowed himself to be drawn into such futility, Michel Lacoste forced his mind back into his dream-world of music. At least there was peace in that beautiful land, where everything was of his own creation. He almost screamed, when this peace was shattered by the raucous shout of swing from the phonograph. He whirled, to see Blanche looking at him in malicious triumph. Something snapped within him. It was more indignity than he could bear.

"Stop it!" he shouted.

Blanche only grinned at him idiotically. With a hoarse snarl, he bounded for the phonograph, wrenched off the record, broke it over his knee. His hard breathing was interrupted by an animal sound from his wife. The room was hot with hatred.

"You bastard!" she screamed and fetched him a stinging smack across the cheek.

Michel's hand came up slowly, as though dragging a heavy weight, rubbed against his reddened cheek. He clawed his hands, and reached out for her blindly, so that she took a step back in terror. Then he seemed to recover his reason, for he dropped his hands, stood looking at the woman for an eternal moment, seeing her for the first time without pity or remorse.

"Michel," she said hoarsely, conscious of what she had drained from him.

Without a word, he turned, picked up his coat and hat woodenly, made for the door. She tried to get between it and him, but he brushed her aside.

"Go on! Kill me! Get it over with!" she pleaded insanely.

The door slammed on her hysteria. She threw it open, panic-stricken for, in her queer way, Michel Lacoste was her love and her life.

"Michel! Michel!"

The empty hall echoed the hollowness in her heart. Blinded with real tears, not all self-pity, the woman closed the door, stumbled across the room. As she threw herself on the chesterfield, she felt a hard lump under her. It was her prescription.

The words leapt at her:

"AN OVERDOSE MIGHT BE FATAL."

She began to laugh and cry at the same time.

There was oblivion in liquor. It blotted out the sound of a woman's nagging tongue. It left nothing but beautiful music running through his brain. He could not forget the torture of an unhealthy blonde face, the unutterable agony of a love lost beyond hope, the terror of a wish to kill.

The bouncer at the last tavern into which he staggered refused him admittance. Michel knew himself very drunk. He poured himself into a taxi, gave the address of Albert Frederick with his last conscious effort.

The butler had gone to bed, and Albert Frederick answered the erratic ringing of the doorbell by the drunken Michel Lacoste. A shadow of annoyance crossed the lawyer's face instantly replaced by a look of concern, as he realized the condition of the young composer.

"Michel!"

Michel sought support from the door-jamb. He hiccoughed, then remembered politeness and placed his hand over his mouth, too late. With what dignity he could gather around himself, he came erect.

"Did you mean it when you said," he asked thickly, "you would put me up at any time?"

"But of course!" Frederick spoke with understanding. "Come in, mon ami."

He assisted the younger man into the library. Michel sank back into an easy-chair. His head lolled against the chair, rolling from side to side as though suddenly broken loose from the spine. His eyes were closed, and he groaned with wretchedness. Frederick watched him with peculiar satisfaction.

"I expected you, Michel, I don't mind telling you. Perhaps not tonight, but soon."

"I *can't* go home."

"It was bound to happen."

"A drink!" Michel tried to focus his bleared eyes. "I need a drink."

"No. You've had too many already. You have a rehearsal in the morning."

"To hell with rehearsals! I need a drink." The eyes closed hopelessly again. "You were right, Albert. I hate her!"

The lawyer considered this with a half-smile.

"You've stood enough from that woman." Frederick played with a paper-match. "Listen, I'll start action immediately."

"Yes!" Michel roused himself slightly. "I must get away from her. If I don't, my friend, I can't answer for what I will do! This afternoon, for the first time, I felt for her—"

"Hatred?"

"It frightened me."

"I can understand that. It is no small thing to think of killing."

"Killing?" Michel succeeded in sitting up. "But no—"

"You are not sure, are you?"

Albert Frederick looked at his drunken protégé for several long seconds. He seemed to be turning something over in his mind, something that was at the same time distasteful and necessary. Finally, he reached a decision, and crossed over to the liquor cabinet.

"You *do* need another drink," he said pouring an oversize slug straight. He picked up the bottle and took it with him, as he gave the drink to Michel. He placed the bottle suggestively by the musician's side. "Drink up!"

Michel swallowed the tumblerful of raw liquid without pause. For a moment, it seemed to revive him. Then the room began to revolve.

"So, you decided to kill her," said Frederick.

The shock of the words pulled Michel together for a little.

"No, no, what are you saying? I decided no such thing! It was rather that *she* killed ... something ... in me."

"I see. What?"

"My pity. I don't feel sorry for her anymore. Can you understand that?"

Frederick refilled the glass. Michel drank more slowly. He felt deathly ill.

"I can understand that you had it in your heart to kill her," said the lawyer with witness-chair relentlessness, planting the seed deeper for later fertile growth. "Isn't that what you just told me?"

Passing a hand over his damp forehead, Michel tried to concentrate.

"No, I couldn't do a thing like that. I couldn't even say it."

"But you thought it. It crossed your mind. For a second you thought it best—"

"Bes' ... to what ...?"

"To eliminate her."

The word blurred on the drunken mind.

"El– elim–elim–"

The effort at concentration was too much. The half-empty glass crashed from nerveless fingers to the floor. Michel made a futile effort to rise. A whirlpool caught him and sucked him under. His head fell against the back of the chair. He began to breathe deeply and noisily.

"Swine!" said Albert Frederick.

The lawyer watched the deadened face for a moment.

"That such a one should create such beauty, while I–" He looked at his manicured hands. "Eh bien, what has been done once can be done again."

He examined the quick plan that had come into his mind, when he had sensed Michel's condition and realized what a violent argument the composer had had with his wife. The plan was good. It left no flaws. There was the record. No doubt the neighbors were familiar with the quarrels. The men of the orchestra. Albert Frederick smiled thinly. Murder is an easy profession.

It had just started to rain. The lawyer laid Michel out on the couch, took off the young man's shoes,

71

covered him with a blanket. After that, he put on Michel's raincoat. Anyone would have said he was Michel from a distance. He walked over to the desk, took out black gloves, put them on. Next, he brought out a gun, pocketed it.

The grandfather clock struck eleven.

Albert Frederick turned out the light and slipped out the door. He heard Michel grunt once, and then cry out in nightmare.

Well, he told himself with a grim chuckle, I will stone two birds with one kill. First, I will bind Michel Lacoste to myself; then we will see whether Mlle. Mary Roberts is as clever as she thinks.

In the darkness, his gloved fingers curved about an imaginary throat. The fingers clenched against the palms, squeezing.

CHAPTER 7

It is no small thing to kill.

Albert Frederick had heard it reasoned that once a man has killed, killing comes more easily. He had even used the argument as a prosecutor.

As he stood outside Michel Lacoste's apartment, listening, the thought seemed to him thin and insubstantial. His breathing was even more rapid than he remembered it from those horrible moments a score of years ago, when his friend's face had turned to him in surprised and pleading terror and then when the roar of the Falls had blotted out all reason and the falling scream had seemed natural, part of the wild landscape and of the ordered scheme of things. His pulse raced beyond normal.

By a great effort of will, Albert Frederick pulled himself together. He was doing the world a favor by ridding it of Blanche Lacoste. She was a nobody, and she wanted to drag Michel down to her level, Michel who could be great in spite of his weaknesses.

There was no sound from the other side of the door. The woman would be sleeping. So much the better for him and for her. The killer inserted the key he had taken from Michel's pocket. Somewhere in the apartments a buzzer sounded, and he knew that meant a visitor at the front doors. He risked more rapid movement, opening the door with a haste he had not planned. The quiet deepened. The killer stepped within the apartment and closed the door gently.

The apartment was as still as a silent prayer. An

electric sign from across the street gave intermittent light. Frederick risked a flashlight, viewed the filthy room with distaste. One more reason for the woman's death. He had only met her one or two times, and each time with a growing lack of cordiality, which he had felt reciprocated. He could regard her impersonally, even inhumanly, as he would an innocent man his eloquence was sending to the gallows.

Blanche was not in the living-room. She must have retired early. He moved softly across to the closed bedroom door, placed his ear against the panel, listened intently. He could hear nothing and was puzzled. Had she, after all, gone out, perhaps with another man? A muscle in his face twitched; the frustration would be too great to bear after he had nerved himself to her murder.

His forehead was cold and damp. He did not like the way his heart hammered. It was proof he was getting older. Yet he felt he had lost none of his cold cunning. He must leave a record in his safety-deposit box on how it felt to murder, particularly to murder for a second time. It would be a shock to the dear old society ladies of Quebec, who worshipped his money and his position and who were forever thrusting marriageable daughters and even granddaughters in his direction. Yes, it was a task to which he must direct his attention. For instance, he could spend many pages explaining how the most careful plans could be led astray by imponderables. If he had been three minutes later tonight, for instance, he might have come face-to-face with whoever had pressed that buzzer down below and whose heavy feet were now mounting the stairs, the feet of someone unconcerned with being seen. It was a thrill and a danger to kill, and there must be a large element of luck, too, he conceded. He had been, would be again, a lucky killer. Dozens of lucky killers walked the streets, free men and women unsuspected, many like himself respected and envied.

74

He thought of Mary Roberts's "whispering city" and chuckled within himself; there were some things the city dared not whisper.

The door gave, as he turned the handle. He waited. Still there was no stir from within. He came into the room boldly, knowing that he could throttle any outcry before it was made. The noise of the gun could be muffled in a pillow.

His flashlight beam picked out the sprawled figure of Blanche Lacoste on the bed. Her arms and legs were somewhat contorted. He could see no movement of her half-exposed chest. He came forward quickly, making more noise than he should have, but still Blanche Lacoste lay inert.

The light glinted on metal. It was a hypodermic syringe. Beside it lay a box. He studied the inscription on the box, without picking it up. His eyes flashed cold fire, and he turned on the lamp on the night-table. His fingers sought the woman's pulse expertly. There was none.

A note was pinned to the pillow beside all that was mortal of Blanche Lacoste. The lawyer unpinned the note carefully, read it, folded it again, and placed it in his breast-pocket. He chuckled horribly.

"You'll have your revenge in a different way than you had dreamed, my Blanche," he told the unhearing-girl. "You must have hated him greatly to have so sold your immortal soul. Perhaps hatred is a sublime force, too."

His keen look took in the night-table once again. There were several empty ampoules, result of poor Blanche's overdose. It must have taken negative courage, he thought, to have injected the liquid from those one by one, knowing that the end was death. He picked up the empty ampoules and placed them in his raincoat pocket. Things could not have worked out better.

"You have saved me a great deal of trouble," he

said ironically to the corpse. "I would not like to have had to kill again."

Yet he had to confess to a vague disappointment.

The police thought the telephone call had come from the concierge. At least, that was the impression that had been left at the precinct station. The janitor denied this vigorously, but he was a notorious liar, and had been in trouble with the police before. It was felt, privately, that he had entered the Lacoste apartment, thinking everyone out, for the purpose of pilfering, but it was obvious he had had nothing to do with the death. The contorted limbs spoke of poison.

Inspector Renault sighed heavily. He was a mild little man, who would have much preferred the priesthood but who had found the examinations at the seminary too exacting. He never became used to violence, and although his compassion was not larger than his duty, he much preferred his garden and his flowers in the quiet summer evening.

"That's right," he said wearily into the 'phone.

"The Blanche Lacoste case. The cause of death is probably an overdose of a sleeping medicine administered by hypodermic. I'd like an analysis of the blood as soon as possible. I am particularly anxious to know how many ampoules would have to be taken to bring about death. Yes, that's right. How soon? Thanks."

Mary Roberts had stood impatiently, while the Inspector spoke into the instrument. She had been fortunate enough (from a newspaper sense) to be at headquarters when the call had come through.

"What time did the woman die, Inspector?" she asked briskly, as he hung up. She held her notebook expectantly.

The policeman looked at her without smiling. Reporters were useful at times in helping the police lay false clues to confuse criminals who could read.

But, in the main, the Inspector looked with jaundiced eyes upon all newshounds, and with particular Gallic disfavour upon female reporters.

"They see too much of life," he would explain to his placid wife, in those night-hours when he was able to be home and they were together in the dark.

"A woman's place is in the home. Now, this little one, Mary Roberts, a comely miss. She would make a bonne femme. Instead, how is it with her? Always chasing after murders with her tongue hanging out. Murders she has on the brain. Although," he conceded amiably, "it must be admitted it is a good brain … for a woman."

So now the Inspector answered Mary Roberts's question without too much cordiality, "Approximately midnight."

"What kind of drug did she use?" the reporter pursued.

"The analysis is being made now. Should know this afternoon."

Mary scribbled, looking altogether too pretty to be also blessed with intelligence. She sensed something more than a suicide behind this. If it were not, her time was wasted, for *L'Information*, in common with most Canadian newspapers, usually omitted suicides from its columns unless of a sensational nature demanding attention.

"And the husband was last seen when, Inspector?"

"Leaving this building about five o'clock yesterday."

A dull-faced detective approached.

"Found this box thrown under the bed," he said.

"St. Louis Pharmacy," his superior read. "Hmmm. Could be something. Let me have it."

While the Inspector dialed the number on the face of the box, the detective added, "There was a whole drawer full of boxes just like that. What the hell kind of a dame was that? Dope?"

Said Mary: "Maybe."

Said the Inspector: "Hold your horses. Don't go jumping them at fences that aren't there. Hullo? St. Louis Pharmacy? Inspector Renault of the Homicide … That's right … Do me a favor please. Check a prescription for me. The number is 837729. No … 29. Yeah. I'd like to know to whom it was issued … hang on."

A detective came along, shuffling some pictures.

"I found some snaps of the dame, chief," he said, holding them out. "She's got sailors with her."

Mary tiptoed over the Inspector's shoulder, as Renault cradled the 'phone with his chin and looked at the pictures. The Inspector clucked his sympathy.

"Jolie! Jolie!" he exclaimed.

"Well, she wasn't so pretty when you took her out of here," said Mary. "Isn't it terrible what married life will do for a woman?"

"How would *you* know? Here, I will loan you these for your paper, but not a word as to their source, you understand?" The telephone came alive at the other end. "Hullo? Yes, I'm still here. That is why I'm able to answer … Made out to 'Mme. Michel Lacoste.' I see. … Picked up by Monsieur Lacoste yesterday about three …. Thank you. Yes, I have the doctor's name. We are checking with him. Thanks for your co-operation. Good-bye."

Renault hung up. He chewed at his full moustache.

"What's your opinion, Inspector?" Mary asked brightly.

"Opinion? Now, why should I have an opinion?" He touched his head significantly. "The neighbors say she was a little–"

Mary was disappointed.

"Then you think it suicide?"

"Ah, you reporters, always looking for murders in simple suicides. Or is a suicide ever simple? To the person involved it must be more complicated than a murder, and as equally devastating. Eh bien–"

"Why doesn't the husband show up?"

Renault managed a sad smile.

"You already have him arrested and hung, have you not, my petite? Ma foi, there could be many reasons why he has not appeared. There seems to have been a quarrel. But we'll find Monsieur Lacoste, of course. I would like to ask him a few questions. Routine, of course."

Mary stamped her foot and said, "Laugh if you want to! For me it was murder."

"Tiens! What did I tell you? I am a crazy one to ask you this, but I ask it nevertheless: what makes you so positive?"

"Look around this apartment!" Mary's brown eyes roamed around the untidy place restlessly. "You're a man, and you wouldn't notice these things, but to a woman it's plain: this woman's housekeeping, her clothes, the romantic trash she reads ... all these prove Mme. Lacoste to have been an exhibitionist and a depressive ... it might be even a manic depressive. She was the kind of woman who always feels sorry for herself. Inspector, where's the note?"

"The note?"

"When that sort of woman commits suicide, she wants an audience, even after death. Ten to one she leaves a note! But in this case, there is no note. No, inspector, for my money it wasn't a suicide."

Regarding her with mock admiration and some grudging affection, Inspector Renault said, "Genius! Sheer genius!"

The girl lit a cigarette.

"I knew you'd laugh at me," she replied composedly. "Okay, Sherlock, don't say I didn't try to help. May I use the 'phone?"

"Sure, it's on the house."

The Inspector went back into the bedroom, and

Mary began to dial the number on her paper. Something caught her eye. She glanced about the room, but no one was looking her way. She replaced the receiver quickly, picked up what had attracted her attention. It was small, even insignificant, yet, of a sudden, it was to her as large and firm as a hangman's noose.

It was one of Albert Frederick's strange match doodles.

CHAPTER 8

When Michel opened his eyes the following morning, he closed them again abruptly. The sunshine hit him like the glare from a tipped Bessemer. A busy little devil used the back of his skull for a xylophone. His mouth felt as though it had been clogged with a fur-boot. He heard someone moving quietly about the floor like a heard of elephants feeding. He forced his eyes open once more.

Albert Frederick was standing over him with a cup of coffee. His involuntary host had a morning newspaper under his arm.

"Michel!" Frederick called crisply, shaking the composer. "Michel! Wake up!"

Michel tried to sit up but the effort was too much for him. Albert supported him into a sitting position.

"Oh, my head!" moaned Michel. "How– how did I get here?"

"That's your least worry now. Here, I brought you some black coffee. Drink up! You'll need it."

The young man drank greedily. The potency and heat of the liquid seemed to overwhelm the invisible xylophonist. His head cleared magically. As it did, the significance of what Albert Frederick had said pen-etrated. He frowned, unable to concentrate as yet.

"My 'least worry,' Albert? I don't understand. What has–"

He broke off, handed the cup back shakily. Certain half-memories, distorted by his hangover, were crowding him.

Frederick said pityingly, "You really don't remember what you told me last night?"

"What I told you?" Michel shook his head too vigorously, so that the xylophonist began an encore. "Oh, my poor head! I'll never do it again, never!"

"Never mind that, now. Try to remember what you told me."

Michel laid his fists against his temples, but it did not seem to help. He gratefully accepted another cup of coffee, swallowed it in a draught.

"Perhaps some tomato juice with worcestershire sauce," he suggested thickly.

The lawyer shook him roughly.

"You'll have to pull yourself together!" he commanded. "Try to recall what you said to me last night."

Words once spoken struggled back into Michel's overloaded brain.

"I said that I had had another quarrel with Blanche," he said tentatively.

"*Quarrel!*" Frederick exploded the word in one small space between them. "You told me you had killed her!"

The grandfather clock was unnaturally loud in Michel's ears. Albert's face became twice life-size in his light. The words the lawyer had spoken rang around in his tortured head like a shout. Then he began to laugh inanely.

"You're joking, of course!"

"Am I?"

The merciless words, the grave pitiless face of the lawyer, had a sobering effect upon young Lacoste.

"Oh, but I couldn't have been drunk enough to say a fool thing like that, Albert!" he protested.

"No? Then supposing you take a look at this."

"This" was the newspaper. Frederick shoved it under Michel's nose, opened at an item. The headline leaped at Michel, blurred, then focused horribly again.

It read:

WIFE OF YOUNG COMPOSER
FOUND DEAD IN APARTMENT.

He glanced feverishly at the opening words:

"Blanche Lacoste, wife of the promising young composer, Michel Lacoste, was found dead this morning in her apartment at …"

Michel threw the paper to the floor.

"Oh no!" he cried. "No! It's all my fault. The poor … oh, Blanche dear, forgive me!"

The horror of his wife's death sobered him completely. Where had he been the night before? What had he done? Had he really said such an insane thing to Albert Frederick? He recalled the time in college when he had had that horrible fight while drunk. He had not been able to remember a thing about it the next morning. He knew he should not drink; he could not "hold his liquor." But what about Blanche? He had not wanted her to die. She had been sick, poor girl, but they had had many good times together, and everything might have worked out if …

He groped blindly for his shoes.

"Where do you think you're going?" Frederick demanded sharply.

"To her."

"You can't help her now," Frederick said.

Michel glanced up at the brutality in the voice. Vague fears poured their vapors into his mind.

"I'm a lawyer. I *know*."

"Albert!" It was a cry. "You don't think *I* did it?"

Frederick began to pace the floor in a first-class simulation of concern.

"What else am I to think? What else will anyone think?" He put a long finger under Michel's nose. "Last night, when you told me, I, of course, didn't believe it. It was too fantastic. I took it to be the liquor talking.

But now–" He gestured at the newspaper. "What do you think yourself, my friend?"

"I couldn't have! I'm not a killer! I couldn't have!"

"Shhh! Keep your voice down. Nobody knows you're here. I gave the butler a day off. Michel, a talent like yours must not be lost to the world. But I must confess to a horror of you, and a fear for my own good sense. A man in my position is supposed to *know* those with whom he deals. I have never been so completely wrong about anyone before. I should have learnt by this time, however, that there is no special stamp upon a murderer."

The final word was too much for Michel Lacoste to bear. He leapt from the couch, waving a fist under his host's nose.

"I am not a murderer!" he shouted. "I have never thought of murder in my life."

"Everyone *thinks* of murder," was the calm response.

"Blanche was all right when I left her. I swear to it!"

"I have never defended a guilty man, yet," said Albert Frederick with his usual cynicism. "Very well, my friend, I will give you an opportunity to prove your statement. Look, I am the crown attorney. I have you on the witness-stand."

Involuntarily, Michel Lacoste shuddered. The knell-like words were accompanied by a complete change in this man who had been such a good friend to him. This was an Albert Frederick he did not know, a demon of a man, with sharp, piercing eyes edging out the truth and a voice that cut and whipped and made miserable jelly of men who thought themselves strong enough for any punishment.

"Let us find out about last night, Monsieur Lacoste," Frederick said, and Michel could see a jury lean forward intently. "When did you leave your wife, Blanche Lacoste?"

Michel thought for a moment, then said, "I think it was around five."

"You *think*. Are you not *sure*?"

"Yes, I'm sure it was five."

"Oh, so now you're sure?"

"Yes."

"Yet not a moment ago, you told me you were *not* sure. Come, come, Monsieur Lacoste. If one has nothing to fear, one does not equivocate."

Michel Lacoste raised a hand, as though to ward off further catechism, but the lawyer went on, "Let us assume that you are certain about the hour of five, Monsieur Lacoste. Where did you go after you left your wife?"

The young man said vaguely, "To a bar."

"'To a bar.' A highly-illuminating answer. And may I ask to which bar it was of the many in Quebec City?"

"Look here, Albert—"

"Answer me!"

"There were a number of them."

"But you just said you went to a bar. Now you say it was to a number of them. You say you are certain it was five o'clock ... at least, you think it was. You have witnesses for all this, Monsieur Lacoste?"

Michel began to cry noisily from grief, for Blanche, from liquor, and from hopelessness.

"You see, mon ami," said Albert Frederick, "your predicament?"

"I—I couldn't be a killer, Albert!"

"Why not? Better men than you are killers."

"But I create; I do not destroy."

"You hated Blanche. You told me so yourself."

"It was just a word."

"An ugly word."

"When a man is drunk, he is not himself."

"Albert—I swear to you— but what's the use? I must

85

do what I can for poor Blanche. She loved life so, even when she pretended to want it least."

Albert Frederick picked up the paper and handed it to his protégé,

"Read the rest of the story," he said. "The police are looking for you. They would like to ask you some questions. Perhaps the same questions I have just asked you, and which you answered so unsatisfactorily."

"Then I'll go to them." Michel reached again for his shoes, picked them up puzzled. "I have nothing to fear–I– These shoes … they're wet."

"That's right."

"But it wasn't raining when I came here. I'm positive of that."

"Another one of your positive statements?" Frederick's face was sympathetic granite, polished. "I'm sorry, Michel. I'd have to testify against that statement. It was pouring when I let you in."

"Pouring?" Michel passed a hand over his eyes. "Are you sure?"

"Yes, I'm afraid that *I* am *sure*."

Michel regarded the shoes stupidly and asked, "At what time was this?"

"At exactly one thirty-five."

"It couldn't have been that late! The last time I looked at my watch, it wasn't much before eleven." His eyes asked the lawyer for help, but there was no help there. A terrible fear came over him, fear of himself and of what he might have done while under the influence of liquor. That fight at the college … the undoubted hatred Blanche had stirred in him last night … "Albert, what did I do between eleven and one-thirty?"

There was a moment of deadly silence. Then the lawyer motioned at the newspaper. Michel shrank from it as though it were a striking cobra.

"No, no, I couldn't have!" he tried to convince

himself, but there was less conviction in his voice. "I couldn't have!"

Frederick turned away from him disgustedly. The lawyer poured himself a cup of coffee, smiling to himself as he did.

"Well," he said, as he stirred, "you'll have to make a decision. Do you want to hang, or are you going to find a way out of this?"

"If I did it, I don't want to live," Michel answered apathetically, but just the same his finger ran around his collar tightly.

"All right." The lawyer sipped. "Go to the police. Tell them you don't remember what you did last night. The neighbours, the orchestra men, will probably have told them already about your frequent quarrels with Blanche. They will have already ascertained that you picked up her prescription at the pharmacy yesterday."

"How did *you* know that?"

Frederick covered his slip quickly with, "You told me. I suppose that's another thing you don't remember? Any self-respecting crown attorney could place a noose of circumstantial evidence about your neck. Even without my testimony, you would be hanged. With my evidence, it would be a foregone conclusion."

The composer moistened dry lips with the thick end of his tongue.

"Please–"

"Have you ever heard the judge pronounce a sentence of death?" Frederick went on relentlessly. "I have. He puts on his black cap. He turns to you, grave and pale. He says: … 'you shall be taken hence to that place from which you came and you shall be hanged by the neck until you are dead.'"

"Stop it! I didn't do it, I tell you!"

"They *all* say that! I watched a man die saying that. It's an old story." He came closer. To Michel, he seemed

87

to fill the room. "Have you ever seen a man hanged? I have. It was early in the morning … dawn. It was cold. That's the way it will be with you. You'll shiver in your thin shirt. You'll love the cold, because you'll know it's the last cold you'll ever feel except the eternal cold. You'll raise your eyes to the patch of sky you'll be able to see, for you'll know you'll never see that sky again, nor hear a bird sing or a child laugh. You'll never again feel a woman's kiss, never again walk in the streets, never again hear the sound of music. …"

"Do you *have* to torture me this way?" Michel burst out. "Not to hear music … not to create it." Tears welled in his eyes. "I committed no crime! Before God, I know I did not. Then why should I hang?"

"But you will!"

"Look, Albert!" He went closer to the lawyer, knowing how the animal in the trap must feel at the approach of the hunter. "You are my friend. You're a great lawyer. You can help me. You can't really believe I did it!"

The taut muscles in Frederick's face relaxed. The victory had been long in coming, the antagonist more durable than he had anticipated. Now, must come the coup de grace …

"What I believe is not of the slightest importance, Michel. But I can help you."

"Thank God. I knew you would!"

Frederick's lips were hard and straight.

"I must warn you, my friend, my fee is high, very high. You might not be prepared to pay it."

The hope went from Michel's eyes.

"You know I'm poor," he said sullenly.

"Oh, I don't need money. I've more money than I require, as you know. I can even afford the luxury to help a struggling young artist to the fame I think he deserves." Albert paused to allow the point to go home. "In my professional capacity, I can snatch that same young man from the gallows. My memory about certain testimony could be convenient. All, as I say, at a price. Unfortunately, this security is threatened by a certain person ... a woman. She is making embarrassing enquiries that need not concern you. I want her eliminated."

The meaning escaped Michel.

"What do you mean ... 'eliminated?'"

"I'm using your own word," said the lawyer. "Don't you remember last night, when you told me you had 'eliminated' Blanche you stumbled over the word?"

A faint recollection stirred within the artist. He shuddered. His face reflected a growing horror.

"You want me to *kill* a woman?" he asked unbelievingly.

"I told you my fee was high, Michel. Besides, what can it matter to you? You have killed once. You cannot be hung twice."

Michel Lacoste looked at his hands. They were strong, good hands, hands to play the piano like an angel. In his brain, there was music. If his neck were broken at the end of a rope. ...

"I am listening," he said dully.

CHAPTER 9

Albert Frederick decided to become ingratiating. He waved at the tray he had brought in, with its toaster and bread and butter and marmalade.

"Help yourself," he said. "Something inside will make you feel better."

"I don't think I could stomach it." The composer's voice was unwontedly harsh. "I've been asked to stomach a great deal in the last little while, and it isn't sitting very well."

The lawyer sat down, crossed his legs, pulled up his trousers neatly, and smiled.

"No need to call spades spades, my friend, when they can be termed instruments for excavating soil." He leaned forward and placed his hand on Michel's knee but drew it away again when he saw it made the young man uncomfortable. "Look, Michel, we've been friends for a long time. We're both in a bad spot. We can help each other. I know I can get you out of the hole you're in. As for this other woman, you don't know her. You would never be suspected in her death. You have no motive. I have a foolproof plan all worked out. Believe me, I am an expert at working out plans. I'll give you all the directions. You won't be caught, I promise you."

Michel's numbed brain failed to respond for a moment to his goading.

"But she's a human being!" he finally blurted out. "And you want me to destroy her!"

"It's she or I ... she or you. ..."

"I'll see you in hell first!"

"No, my friend, it is *you* who will be in hell first. I will merely follow later at my leisure."

Shaken by the sort of fury he had felt in that long-ago age yesterday afternoon with Blanche, Michel could not trust himself to remain in the same room with this man who had such an obscene proposition. He had been dressing, and now he turned towards the door.

"Going out, Michel?" Albert asked pleasantly.

"You're damn right I'm going out! I'm going to the police. I'm going to tell them everything ... including what you just said to me."

Albert Frederick laughed aloud. He kept his hand in his pocket, where the gun-butt was smooth and comforting. If he shot from the pocket at this madman, who could blame him? But it was more imperative that the man become his tool.

"And who will believe a story like that, coming from you, Michel Lacoste? There is no record of our conversation." The face of the lawyer became evil and decadent. "But there *is* a record, don't forget. A little phonograph record made by your dear wife, a woman who, according to her own words, lived in fear of your killing her."

"Albert!"

"It will be a rare jest, will it not? Blanche will have the revenge she thought she craved but never really wanted. From beyond the grave, she will send her husband, the man who murdered her to the gallows! Do you remember? 'To whom it may concern. I, Blanche Lacoste ...'"

Frederick made a suddenly threatening gesture with his pocket, as Michel Lacoste moved with slow menace towards him. "Stand back, Michel! Don't come a step closer! If you do, I'll be forced to kill you! Self-defense, you understand, against a murderer."

"Stop using that word! Stop using it, I say!"

"No need to scream. The neighbours might complain to the police."

"The record?" Michel demanded hoarsely.

"It's in a safe place. It will remain there as long as you behave."

The haze in front of Michel was so red, he was tempted to brave the gun whose obvious outlines bulged this erstwhile friend's pocket.

"You can't use that record against me! You know it was meaningless. I brought it to you myself as a friend, because I–"

"–because you trusted me. And I trusted you – then. Those happy times are over. Now we know each other a lot better."

Michel Lacoste collapsed into the nearest chair with a groan. He buried his head in his hands. When he raised it, he was older, sadder, and wiser.

"Yes, Albert." His voice shook with emotion. "I know you now for what you are. Behind your façade of respectability and benevolence you are a ruthless criminal who will stop at nothing."

"Harsh words, particularly when the pot calls the kettle black. Please try to understand." Frederick seated himself opposite the younger man, and some of the cruelty left his face and his voice was softer and more appealing. "There is all the difference in the world between a first murder and a second one."

"You would know?"

Albert Frederick inclined his head gravely.

"You forget my profession."

"Murdering?"

"There is no call to be sarcastic, my friend. My profession is law. It is my business to consort with criminals, but to never acknowledge even to myself the guilt of a client." He pursued the original thought. "The

92

first time you murder, you think: it's just this one person in my way. Let me get away with it, and I'll pay as long as I live, pay with good deeds, with an impeccable life. Then, one day, someone stumbled on something, and plans to present the old bill again. The second time you shy away from nothing. Well, have you nothing to say?"

Michel asked, "What is there to say?"

"Since I've known you, Michel, I've loved you. I have seen in you the spark of genius I gave my soul to own and found I did not possess. I still love you, Michel; I still want to help you." The voice became cruel and stern again. "But I'll crush you if you don't help me."

"To kill ..." Michel whispered. "To kill in cold blood someone innocent of even knowing you, a woman, perhaps one young and loving live. I couldn't do it Albert, even if I wanted to."

Frederick laughed harshly. There was a singular lack of co-operation in the victim, he told himself wryly.

His voice took on a whiplash sarcasm, as he said, "The wife-killer becomes sensitive about a woman he does not even know! All right, Michel, I wash my hands of the whole affair. *You'll* hang, *I* won't. Make up your mind to that. If you don't rid me of this woman, be sure I'll find some other way. But you'll not live to see it."

"I–I'll have to think it over," Michel said weakly, overwhelmed by the attack and the suddenness with which his simple life had become complicated.

This partial capitulation pleased Albert Frederick. It gave him hope that perhaps he would not have to discard his wonderful plan.

"You do that," he told Michel, making his tone more warm and friendly than it had been. "Go to a cheap hotel, some third-rate place. Stay away from your apartment and your usual haunts.

"Remember that the police will be looking for you everywhere. Register under the name of … let's say … 'Paul Duval.' Yes, Paul Duval is good." He watched, as his suggestions apparently sank home, and Michel Lacoste, picking up his raincoat and hat, made for the door. "Do you need any money?"

"No!" answered Michel Lacoste explosively and slammed the door behind him.

Albert Frederick looked at the closed door with satisfaction. The mouse was nibbling at the cheese.

Michel Lacoste walked the streets of Quebec in a dream. It was a wonder he was not seen a thousand times by the many who knew him. He made no effort at concealment, for he was not conscious of his promenading. He walked by the Chateau Frontenac and past the famous Chien d'Or restaurant, but he had no idea of his surroundings. Thoughts of the dead Blanche and of the perfidy of Albert Frederick hit at his already battered brain. The word "Killer … killer … killer …" came and went on the screen of his mind, always thrust away as an impossibility.

Suddenly, he was struck with dread. A policeman was walking towards him, and he had a feeling he should not be seen by a policeman. His trapped eyes caught a taxi on the other side of the road, and he walked towards it rapidly.

"I want a hotel," he told the driver. "A small hotel not too expensive, you understand?"

The driver grinned.

"Yeah," he said, "get in." He looked off towards the policeman, who was approaching solemnly. "You don't like our friends?"

"Nothing of the sort," retorted Michel, getting in, knowing himself not believed.

In a few minutes, the puffing cab drew up before a place that said "Hotel." The ramshackle building

94

needed something with which it could be identified. It was like a punch-drunk bruiser, dreaming brokenly of better days.

"This do, monsieur?"

Michel nodded. Anything would do where there were four walls within which he could enclose himself to think.

"That'll be four bits."

The composer put his hand automatically in his raincoat pocket. He stopped, poleaxed by the unreality. The driver looked at him curiously, thinking perhaps of a possible reward in connection with this curious young man.

Michel looked stupidly at the objects in the un-clenched hand he withdrew from the pocket. They were six empty ampoules of the sort he had seen Blanche use so often. The evidence was now complete. He had no doubt whatsoever that he had murdered his wife while in a drunken frenzy.

Paying off the driver with a crumpled dollar bill, he walked unseeingly towards the hotel's rickety entrance. Over and over his numbed brain repeated the words of Albert Frederick, "You shall be taken to that place from which you came... and you shall be hanged by the neck until you are dead."

He came to in the dirt-covered "reception room" of the hostelry. A clerk in shirtsleeves was reading *L'Information*. Michel shivered; he might even be reading about Blanche. At last the clerk looked up.

"Well?" he demanded with the hostility of the sort of hired help that does not like to be disturbed in its private pursuits.

"I'd like a room," said Michel.

The clerk grunted.

"Two dollars a day." He glanced down expertly. "No baggage?" Michel shook his head. "In advance."

Michel fumbled for money, paid for three days in advance. The clerk fetched a key from the rack behind him, then shoved the flyspecked register at the new guest. Michel took out his fountain pen, thought for a moment, wrote clearly "Paul Duval" and added after it unhesitatingly, "Montreal."

"Is there a telephone?" he asked.

The clerk jerked his thumb towards a booth behind his desk and went back to his newspaper. Michel walked around to the open-type booth, fished out a nickel, and dialed the number of Albert Frederick. Sweat was in his face, and in his eyes a nameless torture.

"Albert?" He spoke heavily, urging out each syllable. "This is Duval ... Paul Duval ... yes, yes I have decided. Who is this woman you wish me to see? What is her address? What plan do you wish me to follow? ... No, I shall write nothing down. I have a good memory ... when I am not drunk."

He listened for several minutes, tasting the bitterness of hatred.

"Yes," he said finally, "I understand everything. I understand a great deal, now. Everything shall be done the way you wish it. But you must promise to clear me of the other."

Frederick's voice came clearly, "You have my word for it."

"That is charming ... that. The word of one murderer to another. I'll report to you later."

He hung up. The salt of heart-wrung tears was on his face.

"Forgive me, Blanche," he whispered, "for I cannot forgive myself. I am too big a coward to face up to what is coming to me, so I must kill someone innocent."

He stumbled past the clerk.

"Now what the hell," the clerk asked himself, "would a big guy like that be cryin' for?" As a man of the world, he answered his own question, "Dames is no damn good for guys."

The messenger boy scanned the row of cards in the apartment-house address, found the one he wanted, punched the bell. When the buzzer sounded, he opened the door, cakewalked cheerfully up the three flights of stairs to the not-unmelodious accompaniment of his whistle. If guys was goofy enough to send dames flowers, it was none of his business. Well, yes, it *was* his business, but there were dames and Dames.

The girl who answered his ring was instantly classed in his mind as a capitalized "Dame." She gave him a friendly smile, which he returned with an impudent, freckle-faced grin.

"Got a package for Mlle. Roberts," he said.

"I'm Mlle. Roberts," said Mary, holding out her hand, puzzled as to who could be sending her flowers.

"Yeah?" The boy looked her up and down, sceptically started to whistle, checked himself. "You sure?"

"Want to see my birth certificate?" Mary smiled.

"Birthmark would do just the same." The boy ducked in pantomime. "Oops! I keep forgettin' I'm not old enough to say things like that."

Mary Roberts laughed aloud.

"You *don't* forget you're young enough to get away with saying them. I can't think who'd be sending me flowers."

"He's got taste, anyways," said the boy. "Look, you sure you're Mlle. Roberts? He gave me instructions to hand 'em to nobody else?" Mary nodded vigorously. "Okay, sign here."

The girl placed her signature where indicated, took the long box.

"Why'n'tcha open 'em?" asked the boy curiously, keeping his foot in the door.

"You, my delightful little bandit, will either end up in Ottawa or in Bordeaux. You have enough nerve for either a member of parliament or a criminal."

"What's the diff? Go on! Don't be a fraidy-cat. Open up!"

Mary carried the box into the apartment, picked up her purse. She found a stray quarter and took it back to the boy.

"Say," he said, "you're okay. Wait for me, willya?"

"Wait for you?"

"Sure, I'll be old enough in another five years."

He clattered down the stairs, followed by her laughter. Yep, he thought, definitely a Dame.

As Mary turned back to the box of flowers, her heart beat a little faster. She could confess only to herself that her manless state was not a particularly happy one. Under the ribbon with which the box was bound, she found an envelope.

The card in the envelope read:

"Paul Duval."

CHAPTER 10

"PAUL DUVAL."

Mary Roberts knew no "Paul Duval." It was, she regretted, a mistake. She looked at the name on the envelope. It said: "Mlle. Jeanne Robert."

The note read: "To the renewal of our acquaintanceship from my last visit to your city." The writing was firm and masculine, but with the flourish and sensitivity of an artist.

"Now why couldn't it have been me?" Mary asked the ceiling. "Just an unfinished story whispered by my Quebec."

The card gave a telephone number. Mary came to a sudden decision. The flowers would have to be returned, naturally. Such exquisite roses ...

Lighting an inevitable cigarette, Mary looked again at the number on the card, picked up the receiver, dialed. She had to wait quite an interval before a gruff, untidy voice answered.

"I'd like to speak to Monsieur Duval," she said.

"Monsieur Paul Duval."

At the other end the slovenly clerk waved at Michel, who had been sitting for some time in an "easy chair" in the tiny lobby,

"Hey! Here's that call you been waitin' for."

Michel mumbled thanks, as he rose tensely, and went towards the 'phone booth. A pulse in his jaw worked visibly. He picked up the receiver with a damp hand.

"Hullo." He kept his tone reasonably steady. "This is Paul Duval."

The voice that came over the wire to him was young, fresh, and crisp, the voice of someone for whom he felt an instinctive liking.

"Oh, Monsieur Duval, this is Mlle. Roberts," said Mary. "I've just received some beautiful roses with your note. Unfortunately, I'm afraid there's been a mistake. Your flowers have reached the wrong Mlle. Roberts. My name is 'Mary,' not 'Jeanne.'"

Michel tried to play his role lightly and sincerely, saying, "I'm so sorry, Mlle. Roberts. I didn't have the address, and I asked the florist to check it. I hope you will blame him and not me."

"There is no blame, Monsieur Duval," Mary said smilingly. "I am the gainer, for I have had the roses for at least a little while. Would you mind picking them up?"

"Of course not! What is the address, please?"

"I'm at the Chateau Marchand Apartments on Grande Allee."

"The Chateau Marchand Apartments? I'm not too far from you, Mlle. Roberts. I shall be there in a few minutes, if it does not inconvenience you."

"No trouble at all," the girl assured him. "I had no plans. I'll be here all evening. Good-bye."

The man murmured a good-bye and hung up thoughtfully. What was in front of him was even less to his taste than ever.

When Mary Roberts answered the ring of the doorbell, her first impression was of a dark, quick young man of medium height, with broad shoulders and a face that was all eyebrows and troubled smile. The latter she put down to a similar embarrassment to that which she felt. After the light caught him full in the face, she decided he was handsome in a sharp-featured way.

As for Michel, he was unprepared for the petite beauty who confronted him. She was as brunette as Blanche had been blonde, as smiling and brisk as Blanche had been sullen and languid. He was instantly ashamed of himself for even comparing his dead wife with this chance acquaintance whose death he was also to accomplish. The gruesome thought of "also" brought moisture to his upper lip.

"I'm Paul Duval," he stammered. "I just talked to you on the telephone."

"Oh yes, of course, the flowers." She held the door invitingly. "Come in, won't you?"

The impersonator of the non-existent "Paul Duval" took off his hat, and ran his finger around the brim.

"I dislike bothering you—"

"I won't bite." Her ready smile showed two rows of even, white teeth. "And I promise not to take advantage of you."

"I didn't mean—"

"Of course you didn't. Come in, while I get the flowers ready." He stepped diffidently across the threshold, taking off his coat automatically. "I put them in water to keep them fresh. It seemed a shame to let such blooms wilt. They were so lovely that I'm almost sorry my name isn't Jeanne."

It was a flat statement, without coquetry. In another woman, he might have dismissed it but with this dark young girl he felt strangely at home and at ease, as though they were old friends. No other woman had ever given him this feeling, least of all Blanche. He half-followed her into the trim kitchen while she busied herself with the flowers. He remembered Albert Frederick's instructions; however hateful they might be, he had to admit that, from results to date, Frederick was a master of feminine psychology, or at least of this particular woman's psychology,

"Mlle. Roberts, you must forgive me," he said with

every evidence of gallantry. "I'm afraid my mind must have been on other matters, when you telephoned. Otherwise, I would never have suggested this ungallant pursuit of my poor bouquet."

"Don't feel that way. I understand."

"No, please!" He made a deprecating gesture with his hands. "We must leave the flowers where they are. They look perfectly at home. They belong."

"That's very nice of you, indeed, Monsieur Duval." Her large, brown eyes were candidly questioning this dark stranger she found so attractive. "But what about the other Mlle. Roberts?"

Michel shrugged eloquently.

"I have been away for five years. It was not a large friendship. Besides, I cannot seem to locate her, can I?"

"Five years is a long time."

"I am beginning to discover that. I feel like a stranger in my own city."

"You know, I felt the same way when I returned a while ago. But now the feeling has worn off. The city is completely friendly. You won't laugh if I say it whispers to me?"

"I won't laugh. I have heard Quebec whisper as well. To me, it speaks not in words but in music."

"How do you mean?"

More and more he regretted his bargain with Albert Frederick. But it was too late to back out. He remembered the next step he was to take. His hand went to his forehead and he stumbled.

"Monsieur Duval!" the girl called out in concern.

"It is nothing," he protested. "A weak spell. I have not been too well lately."

Mary Roberts urged her chance visitor towards a chair.

"I'll get you a glass of water," she said. "Or perhaps something stronger would be of more help? I have some Scotch."

"That would be more than kind. It will pass in a moment. I know from past experience."

The girl went into the kitchen. He could hear her bustling with glasses and bottles. Dropping his false weakness, he looked narrowly about the room, seeking some further clue to the character of this girl he was pledged to kill.

It was obvious that the apartment had been done over at her suggestion. The decor was modern, but not extremely so, for there was an old-fashioned, quite substantial baby grand piano in one corner. He knew it for a Chickering, as he looked, and his fingers itched. Probably an heirloom, he thought. There were good prints on the walls, and some unpainted bookshelves held books with thoughtful titles. A portable typewriter on a kneehole desk spoke of her profession. Everything in the room held a hint of culture and refinement such as he had yearned to find in the woman he would marry and had thought lost forever in the woman who had been his wife.

At last, his eyes were drawn to the wide windows. He tried to look away but came back to them with a fatal fascination. Those windows, he knew from what Albert Frederick had told him, stood over a sheer drop of some two hundred feet into a rocky ravine. It was from those windows that Mary Roberts, this attractive stranger, was to make a fatal plunge. After he had pushed the girl from the windows, Albert had told him, he was to walk down one flight, wait for the crowd that would pour up the stairs, mingle with it and gradually fade away. Or, if he saw the coast was clear, he could get away through the tradesmen's entrance before the alarm was raised. The death, of course, would be recorded as accidental. It would be surmised that Mlle. Roberts, while admiring the view, of which she was known to be so fond, had leaned too far, had been overcome by dizziness and had fallen. He was to make certain, naturally, to take the card, the envelope, and the floral wrappings with him. He could drop them in the incinerator chute while on his way down the stairs.

Michel stared at his clammy hands in revulsion. They had killed one in anger; now they would murder in cold blood in order that they could be free to go on making music. He balled up his fists in mental agony, squeezing them against his temples.

Suddenly, the desire for music burned within him, as it had done in other moments of crisis. He was drawn irresistibly towards the keyboard of the piano. When he seated himself, and the first vibrant notes of his "Quebec Concerto" flooded from the pulsing strings into the quiet room, it was as though someone had placed kindly hands on his heart and pronounced a benediction. All the sorrow, his loneliness, his pity for Blanche and his hatred for himself and Albert Frederick flowed from his brain to his talented fingers, easing but not removing the pain that was him.

When the first startling notes reached her ears Mary Roberts paused in her errand of mercy. Her patient had obviously recovered, but then she was familiar with the therapeutic value of music. It had often soothed her loneliest moments. What amazed her was the proficiency with which this "Paul Duval" played. She was quite familiar with classical and modern symphonic music, but could not place the music her strange guest was playing. She listened for several moments, shook her head in exasperation with herself for not remembering, and went on mixing the drink. Even if Paul Duval had recovered, he would appreciate the Scotch. And there was a long, dull evening ahead unless …

"Excuse me," he said. "I'm always drawn to piano."

"Please sit down and continue playing," she begged.

"You play beautifully. That is, if you feel well enough …"

"I'm quite recovered thanks."

He actually found himself smiling, almost relaxed, as he accepted the cold glass from her hands. He drank some of it. The liquid warmed him, thawed a bit of the ice about his heart.

"What would you like to hear?" he asked reseating himself.

"Do go on with what you were playing, Monsieur Duval. It's quite lovely. And I must confess to ignorance. It is tantalizing, but I can neither think of the name of the music nor of the composer."

The remark shocked and sobered Michel. He had not realized he was playing his still-unheard concerto. While he began to play again, his brain was busy. He watched the girl, as she smiled whimsically and shook her head.

"I'm sure I should know it, but I don't."

"Do you like it?" He found himself eager for her verdict, when it should not have been of the slightest consequence.

"Very much. Do tell me what it is."

"It's quite unknown so far," he answered truthfully, "but I'm glad you like it."

With natural curiosity, Mary Roberts moved forward to watch the graceful fingers. Michel found her gaze burnt him. He reached the end of the first movement rather painfully, pulled a large handkerchief from his pocket and dabbed at his forehead. The girl misunderstood the gesture.

"It is warm in here, isn't it?" she exclaimed contritely. "I hadn't noticed before, but then I'm—well, a man dresses more. The afternoon sun just pours in!" She moved over to the window. "Come over here. You'll get what breeze there is."

Mary Roberts stood by the open casement window.

The hilltop breeze caught her skirts lazily, molded her fine, short figure. He noted the way her midnight hair lay heavy against her shoulders, waiting for understanding fingers. It made him sick within himself of himself, so that he was physically nauseated.

"You are pale!" she said, with her ready sympathy. "Are you sure you wouldn't like to lie down, while I call a doctor? It could be the heat."

"No, no, it will be quite all right," he told her quickly, alarmed that he might be found here under false pretenses. "As you say, it is warm, and a little air–"

He forced himself to walk over to the window. His feet were lead weights. His heart thumped so loudly he was certain she would hear it and become suspicious. After all, he was a stranger in a beautiful girl's apartment under dubious circumstances. One false move would break the spell he seemed to have unconsciously woven.

As he stood, looking over her at the carpet of the city and beyond, drawing in deep and ostentatious breaths he seemed to hear Albert Frederick's cynical voice in his brain and to know what the lawyer would say in the circumstances: go on, you fool, your chances will never be better; it is all completely natural; get her to lean out to point you out some landmark; then a push on the shoulders, a scream, and it is done. What is an unknown woman to you in comparison with your life? Seize your chance while it is here!

"No!" he said aloud.

"I beg your pardon."

"I was exclaiming at the view," he recovered quickly, not knowing he touched a responsive chord. "It is the finest view of the city I have ever seen."

Mary was pleased. It brought her close to the young man who had come so unaccountably into her life, and whom she had to acknowledge to herself she did not want to see leave.

"Quebec!" she breathed. "My whispering city."

"That's a quaint conceit! But charming. What does it whisper to you, now?"

She gazed mystically over the hazy heights to where Levis stood on the other shore of the St. Lawrence. The compass of her eyes was the city.

"It tells me of a young man who is frightened and lonely," she said.

He drew back, his face a mask.

"I hadn't thought I showed it so freely," he told her stiffly.

"But then I'm a reporter." Her laughter was tender. "You couldn't have known that, could you? A reporter gets to know things, to see behind people."

"And you saw behind me that I was lonely and frightened. I can understand the lonely, but why the frightened?"

"It is something I can't explain. It is only what the city whispers. Perhaps if I were back in New York, it would not be the same. New York is cold, but Quebec is warm. New York has no heart, while Quebec is all heart. There are too many people in New York; there is too little time there. In Quebec there are not too many people, and there is a matter of centuries in which to gather your thoughts and impressions."

He could not explain to himself why he said, "The city whispers to me of you, as well."

"Oh?"

"It tells me that you are lonely, too, and that you are not frightened. You are not frightened, because you love life … greatly."

When it was out, he bit savagely at his cheek wall.

"That's true," she said with her simple honesty. "I find life exciting, always with something new to offer."

The sweat ran down from his armpits in rivulets.

"Can you see the Basilica from here?" he asked

hoarsely, going on, unable to draw back from the fiends that drove him. "I made my confession there as a child."

"Why, of course! It's right over there. The twin spires to the left."

"Where?"

She leaned forward dangerously, having no fear.

"There!" she pointed.

His hands came up slowly, slowly from his sides. He unclenched them with a visible effort, raised them towards her shoulders, which were over the low window edge.

"Yes, yes, I see," he said quickly, to cover his movement.

In a moment, she would go over the ledge. One cry would float back to him. Then would come a sickening sound from the ravine. But he would not have to look or think. He would be moving swiftly, gathering up the evidence. It would be easily five minutes before there was any definite hubbub, even if she was seen to fall. In that time ...

Her shoulders were within three inches of his hands. He braced his feet firmly for the push. The face of Albert Frederick seemed to leer at him. He bunched his shoulder muscles ...

Through his brain shot whole, brilliant bars from his concerto. A man who creates does not destroy. He had said so himself. This young, innocent, lovely girl, to whom Life was a joy ...

Michel Lacoste grasped Mary Roberts roughly at the shoulders. The city spun dizzily below her. She twisted in his grasp with a cry of pure fright.

CHAPTER 11

They stood facing each other, from where he had pulled her back into the room. He swayed slightly, unable to believe what he had done, yet filled with a great joy that he had not killed.

"Monsieur Duval!" she exclaimed, puzzled and hurt.

"You–you will have to for- -forgive me." He could not control his tongue or his beating heart. "I have acrophobia ... fear of heights ... I cannot stand to see anyone lean out of a window ... I must pull whoever it is back."

"Oh!" The relief was patent in her voice. "For a moment I thought–"

She thrust the idea that he had been going to push her out of the window from her mind as absurd. Victims of acrophobia, she knew, could not bear to have anyone else lean over heights. She had seen one who had jumped from the Quebec Bridge ...

"Yes?"

"I thought you had fallen against me in a faint," she finished glibly. "You must sit down and rest."

Michel became queerly agitated.

"I must leave immediately," he said almost roughly.

"But–"

"Really! Please don't try to stop me. I can't explain, now."

The masquerader was in a fury to go.

"You're a strange man," said Mary, somewhat settled. "I thought–"

"You thought what?" Michel bit back.

"Well, frankly, I was enjoying this. I felt that you were, too. Is it wrong of me to be so bold?"

He was at the door and had it half-open. He turned, scarcely trusting himself to speak.

"You—you could do no wrong!" he said huskily, and shot out the door.

She stared unhappily at where he had been, and wondered whether she would ever see him again. At least, he had left the roses.

Mary went back into the kitchen and picked up one of the fragrant blooms. She held it reflectively to her nose. It reminded her, for some unfathomable reason, of the man she knew as Paul Duval.

Shrugging, she went back to her typewriter to smother rekindled hopes in work.

Deslauriers had waited an hour for Michel Lacoste, then had engaged a substitute solo piano and gone grimly ahead with the rehearsal of the "Quebec Concerto." The world premiere had been advertised. Bien! It would proceed! These artists!

High on the narrow gallery that led to the catwalk along the flies, a solitary figure hunched, completely absorbed in the music. From time to time, the figure made impatient moves as though dissatisfied. From out of the darkness, a hand fell on the figure's shoulder and it whirled in panic.

"I thought I'd find you here, Michel," said Albert Frederick.

The breath whistled back into Michel's body. The triphammer pounding of his heart lessened.

"You might have given me some warning," Michel said sullenly.

"Fearing the grasp of the Law?" The lawyer smiled pleasantly, and seated himself beside his protégé. "It's very foolish for you to come here, my friend. I'm not the only person to whom it might occur to look for you here."

"I had to chance it, Albert. I *had* to hear what they were doing with my music. I watched my chance to sneak in."

"Well, it's done, anyway. Listen–"

Michel grabbed the lawyer's arm roughly, as the orchestra began the second movement again.

"Quiet!" he said. "I want to hear this."

They listened in their incongruous manner until the conductor called a "break." Frederick's tense enthusiasm was as great as that of the concerto's creator.

"Beautiful! Beautiful!" he said at last. "It's by far the best thing you've done, Michel."

"Yes, yes, it is." Michel groped for words. "I feel as though I were on the threshold of some great achievement."

It seemed to him absurd that his knees trembled where he clasped them with his hands.

"It would be a pity," said Frederick, a smooth threat in his tone, "if anything should happen to take the savor from your triumph."

"Never mind that!" Michel answered harshly.

"Oh, but I must! You see, I have a stake in both these things myself. Did you meet her?"

"Yes," came the bitter answer, "I met the lamb who is threatening the lion."

"Do not let the lamb pull the wool over your eyes," smiled the lawyer. "Likewise, do not twist the lion's tail."

Michel was silent for so long a time that Frederick became uneasy.

"What happened?" he snapped. "You haven't– already?"

"No, I haven't. I did exactly what you suggested. But– I had no … opportunity."

Frederick did not perceive the reason for the hesitation, thinking it a natural repugnance for the subject.

He did not like to think himself of that vibrant young girl dying, but the law of self-preservation was over-developed in him.

"Did she receive you well?"

"Extremely so."

"Ah!" It was a sound of satisfaction Michel found distasteful. "Then you will be able to arrange another ... meeting?"

"I think so. She seemed reluctant to have me leave."

Frederick rubbed his hands together in the gloom.

"Good! Good! It is exactly as I had anticipated." He became quite jovial. "You are an attractive fellow, Michel."

"Oh, shut up!"

"Come, there is no offense at a compliment. How soon do you think you will be able to see the girl again?"

"I—"

"Tomorrow?"

"I suppose it could be arranged."

"Then let's make it tomorrow, by all means. I have an important case in court all day, which will give me a perfect alibi, if ever one is needed."

"Your skin comes first, of course," the young man sneered.

"You're in a churlish mood, indeed! My skin happens to have the value of a rare curio to me."

"Well?"

"I have checked with the meteorological bureau by telephone. The weather will be fine."

"So now it's weather reports—!"

"Now, now," Albert Frederick chided, "we are difficult, aren't we?"

"Well, what in the name of St. Joseph has the weather to do with an assignation for murder?"

"The young lady has an automobile. It will be a

112

nice afternoon for driving. You will, as a visitor, want to see some of the points of interest. For instance, Montmorency Falls."

"No!"

"Oh, but yes! Do you know the Falls at all?"

"I have climbed the cliffs many times."

"Then you will climb them once again, this time in the company of Mlle. Roberts."

"Oh …"

"You see, Michel, it is eminently simple. No muss, no fuss. A little push, and voilà! It is done. The Montmorency Falls have great scenic beauty. Higher than Niagara. They are also straight down … and once a human being goes into their boiling depths … well, what kind of a human being comes out?"

Michel was glad Albert could not see his face, for he knew that he wanted with all his heart to kill this man who talked so calmly of murder.

"Also, on a weekday, the Falls are lonely and deserted. A couple could climb those heights and never meet anyone else. You will make certain you are not seen. It would be awkward, if, for example, you had to testify at the inquest and your real name came out, as it undoubtedly would." Albert Frederick broke off with an exclamation. "How curious! If I'm not mistaken there is the subject of our conversation, now."

Following Frederick's pointing finger down onto the stage, where the orchestra was resuming its seats, Michel Lacoste stared in undisguised amazement and alarm to where the petite Mary Roberts was standing talking to Auberge, the impresario.

"How could that be?" he frowned. "What's she doing here?"

"Do you think she recognized you, and was only leading you on to see what you would do?"

"Why should she? I never saw her before today. I'm worried."

"No need to be, my friend." Frederick professed a calmness he did not feel. "I'm certain it is nothing but a co-incidence. After all, she may have been assigned to do a story for her paper about your forthcoming concerto. It will have more news value, in view of what happened to your wife and your strange disappearance."

It is lucky, Michel thought, that he cannot see within my mind, or he would be worried, too. Why should I, a supposedly hunted man, a man pledged to kill a woman, suddenly find his heart beat faster at the sight of that woman, and not from fear but from a strange sense of comradeship? I must put such thoughts from me, or I will never know peace.

The harried young man forgot everything, as Deslauriers rapped for attention.

"Off the top," said the conductor, "and let's have a complete run-through without an error, if possible. On the downbeat, gentlemen."

The "Quebec Concerto" began.

If he had but known, Albert Frederick was prescient. It was, indeed, a co-incidence that Mary Roberts should be present at the rehearsal of the concerto. Monsieur Durant, whose nose for news was far superior to his memory for the whereabouts of spectacles, had sensed the drama in the rehearsal of a composer's new work, while the police were looking for that composer "for questioning."

"I would like to interview Monsieur Deslauriers," she had told Auberge.

The impresario did not know whether to be flattered or anxious. Space in *L'Information* could sell seats; it could also have an adverse effect upon the box office. He decided to take a chance, and let the interview go through. As he made up his mind, the music started.

"I'm sorry," he said, "but you'll have to wait until the run-through of the concerto is complete. The re-

114

hearsal costs scale, you understand?"

"That's all right," said Mary. "It'll give me a chance to hear the music. I'm told it's something special."

"We believe so." Monsieur Auberge smiled. "But then, perhaps, we are prejudiced. Would you like to sit in the orchestra until it is all over? You can have any seat in the house, now! I hope the night of the concert vacancies will be at a premium."

Mary laughed understandingly and made her way to a seat in the shadows about halfway back. She did not know that the cold eyes of Albert Frederick followed her in appraisal.

As she listened, Mary was conscious of a growing uneasiness. She could lay no finger on the reason for this, until, of a sudden, the music became terrifyingly familiar.

It was beyond belief, but this was the same music that had been played on her piano in her apartment by the man who called himself Paul Duval. Yet, if the music had not had its world premiere, who would know it well enough to play by heart? Paul Duval? But Paul Duval, from his own story, had lately come from Montreal. Michel Lacoste? Who else? It was certainly nobody from the orchestra, nor was it the solo pianist.

The blood constricted around her heart. Why should Michel Lacoste, if it was Michel Lacoste, masquerade under another name and make such an elaborate pretense (for pretense it must have been) in order to make her acquaintance? Surely a man wanted by the police did not seek blind dates by such extraordinary means without some reason? A wisp of information blew about her brain but she could not catch it.

Monsieur Auberge came out and sat beside her. He noticed her intense interest in the music.

"Magnifique, n'est-ce pas, Mlle. Roberts?"

She nodded, still chasing that wisp. Could it be …

115

"Tell me, Monsieur Auberge, who is the angel of this concert?"

The impresario smiled the satisfied smile of a man who knows he cannot lose on a gamble.

"Why," he answered, "a man who is truly an angel, Monsieur Albert Frederick, the lawyer. I would appreciate your giving his generosity and appreciation of the Arts a mention."

"You may rest assured," said Mary Roberts, "that I will do everything in my power to make Monsieur Albert Frederick truly angelic."

CHAPTER 12

It was easy for Monsieur Durant to see that his favourite girl reporter was excited. The very springiness of her walk, as she came into his office, told him more than a half-column statement.

"So," he said quizzically, pushing up his spectacles, "the concerto is good, no?"

"The concerto is good, yes." Mary Roberts sat on the edge of the editor's desk, one shapely leg swinging in fast time with her thoughts. "So's the story onto which I think I've stumbled."

"More murders?"

"Please don't tease me, Monsieur Durant! I think I've really got something hot, if my hunch is right. Have we a picture of Michel Lacoste, a recent one?"

Durant nodded.

"One came this morning from the publicity man at the Opera House. I had it held up, because I thought we might use it for more than a publicity yarn." He rummaged around in a pile of photos, came up at last with the one he sought. "Here it is."

He handed Mary a photograph. One look was enough to tell her that this was a photograph of the man who had called her at her apartment, using the name "Paul Duval." She shuddered as she thought of that episode at the window. Could it have been that he was suffering from acrophobia, or that he had …? Yet, he was so attractive and obviously upset. Was he really responsible for his wife's death? She told herself "no," fiercely. What was his tie-up with Albert Frederick?

Was he a willing tool of that horrible man? Surely, unwilling!

"I have seen this man," she said to Durant with tantalizing slowness.

The laziness left the editor's manner. He sat up straight in his chair, and his eyes were no longer mild.

"Well?" he barked.

"He was in my apartment last night … having a drink."

"What! Michel Lacoste in your apartment? You're joking! What was he doing there?"

"Passing himself off as a probably non-existent person known as 'Paul Duval.'"

"In the name of heaven, woman!" Durant exclaimed. "What kind of fire are you playing with? The police are looking for that man."

He reached for the telephone, but Mary laid a hand imperatively on his arm.

"Please, sir, there's a lot behind this I don't understand."

"Nor I!"

"But what can you tell the police? That he visited me? It does not find Michel Lacoste for them. I have another feeling: that Michel Lacoste will return."

Durant snorted, "Women's intuition, I suppose!"

"Call it that if you want. What a feather, then, for *L'Information*, if this paper turns Michel Lacoste over to the police."

A gleam came in the managing editor's eye, but it went quickly.

"Non, ma petite, that may be all right for New York, but not in Quebec City. Besides, think of the risk."

"My insurance is all paid up."

Durant smiled in spite of himself.

"Believe it or not, Mary, I was a reporter once

118

myself, even a cub. Sometimes I think our journalism has grown too staid, too polished, too sure of itself. We need some of the 'Front Page' again. It wouldn't hurt once in a while to go back to the bad old days of reporting, when it was every man for himself and a pink slip in your pay-envelope if you got scooped by the opposition. Why, today, with wire services and everything …"

He broke off and smiled sheepishly.

"We all grow old," he ended. "No, Mary, I cannot let you do it. If anything happened to you on such a mad venture, I would never forgive myself."

"You forget my classification as marksman."

Durant had forgotten. He thought of his dainty reporter's snub-nosed .32 and the target she had once shown him, shot on the police range with that weapon, a perfect cluster of bull's-eyes. Even the chief of police had remarked to him upon the girl's unusual proficiency.

"Annie Oakley could outshoot any man alive," Mary had told him with feminine placidity.

"I'll tell you something else," Mary pursued her advantage. "I don't think Michel Lacoste is a murderer at all."

"Oh? More feminine intuition? You women must always throw in your feelings against logic and facts. That's a fraud. It constitutes an infringement of the male right to be always correct."

Mary was huffed.

"If you're going to make a joke of it, Monsieur Durant–"

"Now, wait, don't get on your high horse. Let's think this through clearly. Just what do you hope to attain?"

"A story for *L'Information* … exclusive."

"I see." The editor grinned wolfishly. "And that is clear thinking? A story … exclusive? Damn it all, woman, that's the one argument that would have won me, and you know it! Who is your beneficiary?"

"You, Monsieur Durant," she answered sweetly. "And don't bother to have another reporter or a detective tail me. I'll give anyone who tries the slip. You know I can do it, too."

The editor shook his head after her in some bewilderment. So much feminine charm running around on such nice legs should not be so efficient and possessed of that pistol in the handbag. Ah well! Monsieur Durant went back to his page one makeup problem.

It had been a simple matter for Mary Roberts to telephone the number "Paul Duval" had left, ask the address of the surly person who answered the telephone, and present herself at the desk of the rundown hotel. As she looked with distaste at her surroundings, she realized that her quarry had chosen his hiding-place well.

Mary had little of a plan in her mind. Her thought was to get this man away to some place where they could be alone, always trusting to the pistol in her handbag. Her car was outside, and it was a nice day. That was as far as her thinking had gone.

"Is Monsieur Duval in?" she asked the slovenly clerk, who was at his usual occupation of reading a newspaper left behind by one of the guests who could afford the three cents.

The clerk did not bother to look up.

"Number thirteen," he said. "Upstairs."

Mary looked up the gloomy flight of stairs, her confidence leaving her.

"Couldn't you," she asked timidly, "couldn't you just let him know I'm here–"

Giving her a "look," the clerk shouted up the well, "Hey, Number Thirteen! There's a lady wants to see you in the lobby!"

He seemed to go back to his paper, but Mary felt uncomfortably that his eyes were on her. She, in turn, could not help looking with apprehension at the misery of the place in which "Paul Duval" had chosen to live, the faded, peeling wallpaper, the holes in the worn carpet, the frayed upholstery of the two chairs in the lobby.

"Yeah!" said the clerk belligerently. "It ain't the Ritz!"

Feet clattered down the uncarpeted stairs. They halted near the bottom, as a man would do who was looking for trouble, then they came forward again eagerly.

"Hullo!" said Michel. "It's you!"

The way he said it was almost boyish.

"I hope I'm not disturbing you, Monsieur Duval."

The clerk grunted and went back to his newspaper. They moved as far away from him as possible in the small place.

"Not in the least," Michel said, and added ironically, "As you can see by the splendor of this place, I'm not working."

"But you could afford roses?" she asked innocently.

He stiffened and said with some hostility, "Why did you come here?"

"I came to see you."

"About what?"

She thought his jaw very set, his eyes haunted and suspicious.

"About yourself."

"I don't see–"

"Monsieur Duval!" She laid an impulsive hand on his arm. "You left my apartment so abruptly, there was such an expression on your face … I– had to see you again."

The lovely girl sounded so sincere he was touched. That she should venture into such surroundings as he had chosen was doubly a compliment. Nevertheless, he shook off her hand.

"Go away from me!" he said harshly. "I'm not fit company for you."

"Let me be the judge of that."

"All right, what do you want?"

"Please don't be bitter. I thought perhaps you needed someone to talk to." She smiled. "I'm a good listener."

Michel returned the smile without reserve, his face suddenly lighting attractively.

"So I noticed."

"Oh, not only for music, Monsieur Duval. As you know, I listen for a living."

"Yes, of course, you're a newspaperwoman." He hesitated, then grimaced. "You think perhaps I'm material for a human interest story?"

"Don't put it as badly as that—"

Michel shrugged his shoulders.

"Maybe you're right, mademoiselle. It might be a great relief to talk to you."

"You know what?" asked Mary eagerly, as if she had just thought of it. "We can take my car, go for a ride in the country."

He was startled.

"Why the country?"

"Why not?" Her laughter showed her dimples. "Are you a back-seat driver? If you are, I'll let you drive. You can show me the places you like best."

Won't you stop throwing yourself at me? Michel thought frantically. Why do you put everything in my way? I don't want to do anything to you. You're too lovely, too sweet. But you're driving me to it. No, you're offering to let me drive you to it.

"On such a beautiful day," he said aloud, "with such a beautiful companion, the offer is too tempting to be turned down."

122

"Then let's start right now! We can get lunch along the way."

He threw everything away in which he had ever believed. This time he would go through with it.

"All right," he said. "I've got a 'phone call to make and then–"

"About a job, maybe?"

"Yes, about a job," he answered slowly. "I don't know whether I want it or not, but I guess I'll have to take it. Beggars can't be choosers. Excuse me, please."

He walked quickly to the telephone booth, as though to stay would make him change his mind. His finger was clumsy as it dialled Albert Frederick's number. He watched the girl through the glass of the partition. She was applying lipstick. Her handbag was open. In it lay a small-calibre automatic. The other party answered.

"Hullo, Frederick?" He paused, sucked in a deep breath, went on steadily. "We're leaving for Montmorency ... how do you expect me to feel?"

The receiver suddenly had the touch of a live snake, and he banged it back into place. A roar like that of a tumbling falls was in his ears.

CHAPTER 13

The roadster was as cute as Mary. Michel could not help thinking, as he urged its trim little chassis along the highway, how Blanche would have enjoyed riding in it, and how she would have envied and villified the girl beside him.

They drove through picturesque scenery with the gaiety of tourists. Each had thoughts.

… It will only take a small push, Michel was thinking, because she is such a little person. I must get that gun away from her, somehow. I must make sure we are alone. The gun will have to go over the Falls, too. She is so charming and so sincere. If it had been her, instead of Blanche, I would not be on this fateful ride. But that is the way it is with Life …

… I must watch his every move, Mary Roberts was thinking. Of course, I could be mistaken in everything, but I can't take any chances. What will he do? Will it be an accident in the car? Or will he take me to some remote spot? Am I chasing a mirage, or am I really riding with a murderer? No, I've made up my mind, he's too nice, too sincere, to be a killer. But Albert Frederick has some hold upon him. Why did he come to visit me? Did he pull me back from the window of my apartment, or was he pushing me? Am I a damn fool, and should I hail the nearest policeman? The gun is good insurance …

On the surface, they were even happy. It was a grand day, with a little nip in the breeze that they did not seem to notice.

Mary noticed none of this. All this beauty had become ugliness to her, the grim visage of Death. She was young, she had told him, and she loved life. Yet, as he came towards her with curving hands, there was no pity in his face, but rather a set of anguish as of a man who had to drown kittens when he likes kittens.

"You're not dizzy?" he asked hoarsely.

She shook her head, not trusting herself to speak. Her gaze went around the whole top. It was empty and forlorn. A gull wheeled, screeching overhead, then beat strong wings against the breeze back to the St. Lawrence.

"It's far down, isn't it, Mlle. Roberts?"

If he came a step nearer …

"Why are you so pale?"

"This place, Monsieur Duval … it's deserted."

"Yes. We seem to be the only ones loafing on a weekday."

Why did he smile so? It was a fixed and horrible grin. She had noticed it on the face of a man who was to be hanged the following day and for whom reprieve had been denied.

"Don't go too near the edge," he warned.

Her spirits came back fighting.

"Have you perhaps rediscovered your acrophobia, Monsieur Duval?"

"I see. You have been doing some thinking. Thinking is dangerous, mademoiselle."

"But sometimes profitable–" Mary Roberts decided to plunge, "–Michel Lacoste!"

The last bit of color fled from his face. He was left paper-white and shaken.

"You– you knew?"

"Of course! And I told my office where I was going."

His knees began to tremble. Rage crept up his spine and into his working hands.

"That's a lie! You didn't know where you were going!"

"I had a pretty good idea." She could not tell whether her desperate bluff was working. "I had a good idea from what happened with Albert Frederick twenty years ago on this same spot.

It was like a punch to the solar plexus.

"You—you mean—"

"Twenty years ago, Robert Marchand went screaming from these heights into the Falls. He was pushed by Albert Frederick, but of course, it was an 'accident.' Just as I am to be an 'accident.'"

"Shut up!" he commanded thickly. "Shut up!"

"I don't believe you're a murderer, Michel Lacoste," she went on quickly, "I believe you are the victim of some plot by Albert Frederick."

"Blanche is dead!"

"But not by your hand, of that I am sure!"

It worked around in his enflamed brain, but he could not make the conviction of the truth of what she was speaking rise. To save himself, he would have to kill again. A great struggle went on within him, the ever-present inward fight of man between his good and his evil intensified to the point of hysteria.

"Let us talk it over," she pleaded, taking a backward step.

She could go no farther. Her feet were on the slimed brick of the Falls. The roar in her ears made her dizzy and confused.

"There is nothing to talk about."

"Oh, but there is! You must believe me. For my sake and for your own, you must! You don't want my blood on your hands!"

He looked at his hands as she said that. He looked at them as though they did not belong to him, as though they were disembodied, not operated by his will.

Mary Roberts cried out, "Listen! Do you know what I found in your apartment the morning after your wife died? I found a doodle. It was the kind of doodle with paper matches that only Albert Frederick makes."

The man who had to murder to live waited.

"I have the match here, in my pocket. Look!"

Her hand dived into her pocket. As it encountered emptiness, a look of unmitigated horror transformed her lovely face into unrelieved ugliness.

"Please—" she croaked. "Please—"

"You have lost something?" he asked almost pleasantly. "Perhaps this?"

In the flat of his outstretched hand lay her automatic.

"I took the liberty of relieving you of it back there." The false gaiety left his face. It became a mask of graven stone. "And now, perhaps—"

He hurtled the gun into the abyss.

"You will have no need for it, Mlle. Roberts. Of that, I can assure you. Shall we finish with the business?"

Michel Lacoste took a quick step towards the girl he had been ordered to murder.

She screamed.

The cry of great and hopeless terror was lost in the pitiless clamor of the descending waters.

CHAPTER 14

The newspaper in Albert Frederick's hand shook ever so slightly. He tried to gaze out the window, but was attracted back to the heading under his index finger:

"GIRL REPORTER KILLED IN PLUNGE FROM TOP OF MONTMORENCY FALLS
Mary Roberts, aged 23, of New York City, reporter on the staff of *L'Information*, fell to her death, while apparently engaged in a lone sight-seeing tour of famed Montmorency Falls. The body of the attractive young woman, who was well-liked by all her associates, has not yet been recovered. Coroner Dr. Ludwig Gagnon was of the opinion that an inquest would not be necessary, but postponed official decision until the body of Mlle. Roberts was found."

The story went on for two more paragraphs under the two-column head, praising the work of the late Mlle. Roberts, and ending with a tribute from the Chief of Police.

The lawyer took a deep breath, and his heart felt lighter than it had in days. At last he was free again, an intolerable shadow lifted from his happiness. And all quite naturally, without any fuss, and with no personal involvement. Albert Frederick laid down his newspaper and faced his visitor.

"Relax, mon ami," he said, noting Michel Lacoste's perturbation. "Your worries are over. So are mine."

He got up and went towards Michel, but the composer shied away from him. Frederick shrugged, went to the liquor cabinet.

"A toast, Michel?"

There was no answer. Frederick faced around in his best courteous manner.

"Look, it was an accident. You never knew her. It's something you read in the paper. Tomorrow it will be forgotten, like a bad dream."

Michel Lacoste continued to look at the lawyer oddly, as a noisome slug brought to light when a rock turned over. Frederick tossed off his drink, affecting not to notice that Michel had refused his.

"I paid my fee!" Michel's voice came queer and harsh, a man forcing himself to speak to someone he despises. "Now, deliver your service to your client. How are you going to save me from the consequences of what I did to my wife?"

Placing the tops of his fingers together carefully, Albert Frederick considered the remark.

"You don't think I'd cheat you?" he asked calmly.

"I wouldn't put anything past you!"

Their eyes crossed swords. It was Frederick's that fell away first. He was glad that the ringing of the telephone gave him excuse to turn away entirely. He scooped up the receiver. It was the switchboard of *L'Information*.

"Why yes," he said, "I'm always in for my old friend Durant ... Hullo, Edward ... Help you with a statement on the Patterson case? Why certainly, I'd be honoured ... In your office tonight? Well, if you say so ... Seven-thirty. Right, I'll be there."

He went to hang up, but the voice on the other end crackled on. "No, you don't say! I hadn't seen the newspaper. ... Yes, it's so tragic. But then we all have to go some time. ... Yes, I'll be there for sure."

He hung up, looking thoughtful.

"Poor old Durant," he said at last. "He liked that girl."

Should I tell him that I did, too, Michel Lacoste thought fiercely? That I still do? How I hate the slimy ...

"I'm waiting for my reward," said Michel, keeping his voice lifeless to hide his hatred.

"It is very simple, Michel. You see, I was in your apartment the night Blanche died."

The composer sat, carved from stone. Albert Frederick, who had hoped to enjoy a cat-and-mouse game, was obviously disappointed.

"I'm surprised at nothing coming from you!"

There was such venom in the voice of his erstwhile protégé, that Frederick stepped back. He made his quick way around his desk, opened a drawer, put a hand on a revolver there. The feel of it brought back his assurance. Michel suddenly pointed an accusing finger at his patron.

"You killed her!" the musician blazed. "You killed Blanche! I should have guessed ... before ... before ..."

"Wait, Michel! Don't come any nearer! Listen to me, my friend. I can prove that I didn't kill your wife. I can prove it by the same means that I can show you didn't."

Michel looked at him incredulously.

"You mean–"

Frederick cut him off with a gesture. He opened a secret drawer in his desk, and brought out Blanche's suicide letter. He tossed it across the desk.

"Read that."

Tearing out the letter the envelope contained, Michel read feverishly. Mingled doubt, surprise, and relief were reflected on his expressive countenance.

"What–where–"

Frederick kept his hand on the hidden gun and said, "I found it the night your wife committed suicide.

134

It was pinned to her pillow. I'm certain you'll recognize your wife's handwriting, not to speak of her style. The police will be able to verify these readily, no doubt. I can destroy the record, which did not mean anything without my testimony, anyway."

Michel's face was haunted.

"Then I didn't kill her," he whispered, and, as certain memories overtook him, "Poor, poor Blanche."

He put his note in the pocket mechanically. Only part of his brain seemed to be working. Then, apparently, another shocking realization reached his nerve centres. Hate transmuted his face beyond all recognition.

"You made me believe I was a killer," Michel said through his teeth, "so that I might kill for you?"

"It was necessary that I secure your co-operation," Frederick answered suavely. "And it was as I told you … a second murder is so much easier…."

"Aren't you afraid it might become a habit?" asked the composer. He went to the door abruptly. "I'd better leave."

The lawyer watched him go with deep regret. He hated to lose a friend, particularly a friend he regarded as a genius.

"Poor Michel," he said softly to the walls of his library, "it has been hard for you. It is not easy to kill." His mind's eye turned inwards. "At least, you will be able to take out your night of horror in your music. While I–"

He poured himself another drink.

When Albert Frederick came to *L'Information*, it was night. Most of the office was in darkness. A lone boy was in attendance. The door was locked, and the lawyer rapped sharply. It took seconds for the boy to struggle awake.

135

"One moment," the boy called, and fumbled with the key in the lock with sleepy hands. At last the door yielded.

Frederick was a little put out at the delay.

"Is Monsieur Durant in?" he asked abruptly. "He is expecting me– Monsieur Frederick."

"Oh yes, sir! He asked me to apologize. He has been delayed for a few minutes, but will be back at any time. He asked me to have you wait for him in his office. I'll show you where it is."

The lawyer waved him back to his chair.

"I'll find my own way. I've been here often. You go back to sleep. At your age, one needs a lot of sleep."

The boy smiled sheepishly, and settled himself more firmly in his creaking chair. Frederick went ahead into the dim cityroom. It was usually so alive that it had a peculiarly disquieting air in its present dark stillness. Albert was not a nervy man, but he glanced around several times, until he reached the door of the managing editor's office. As he put his hand on the doorknob, a thought struck him.

He turned and looked around the cityroom. His searching gaze stopped at a desk. A neat sign on the desk read "MARY ROBERTS." It had been so soon after her death that her effects had not yet been touched. Perhaps the police had issued orders to leave things exactly as they were.

The diary the girl had taken from Renée Brancourt's rooms must be in her desk. It was not in her apartment. He had made certain of that.

Making sure that the boy on guard had fallen asleep, Albert Frederick went quietly to the desk. With that diary out of the way the last shred of evidence against him would be destroyed. He would sleep of nights as he had not slept in years.

As he leaned over the desk, Mary Roberts' young

and alert voice said distinctly, "You won't find the diary in there."

The hand reaching to open one of the desk drawers stopped as if against an invisible wall. Albert Frederick whirled. He was alone. The cityroom was deserted.

"I must pull myself together," Frederick thought. "I have heard Robert Marchand's voice so often in my imagination. Surely, it is not to be repeated with this girl, killed by another!"

He felt the sudden need of a drink. Perhaps Durant had something in his office.

It was while he was seated in Durant's office that he saw the girl. He looked up, and there she was, passing from one shadow to another, not too distinct. He blinked, but the vision did not go away. Rather it seemed to slowly dematerialize, much as though Mary Roberts passed from one dimension to another.

Albert Frederick was not lacking in courage. He dashed for the office door. By the time he had wrenched it open there was nothing in the cityroom but poor light and waiting shadows. He ran through the cityroom to the outer office, shook the attendant awake roughly.

"The girl!" he demanded hoarsely. "Where'd the girl go?"

"Girl?" The boy looked about sleepily. "What girl, Monsieur?"

"There was a woman in here."

"There's been nobody in here but you and me, Monsieur. Look for yourself! The door is still locked."

The lawyer's hand was clawlike on the door, when a key scraped in the outer lock. He drew back from the door, and Durant bustled in.

"Ah, Albert," said the editor, "sorry to keep you waiting."

With a great effort, Albert Frederick pulled himself together.

"It's all right. I've only been here a few minutes."

Frederick began to regain control of himself. He knew about hallucinations and considered now that he had been the victim of one. But his naturally pale face was unhealthy.

"I won't keep you for long," said Durant. "Good of you to come, my friend." He seemed to notice the lawyer's harried appearance for the first time.

"Anything wrong? You look upset."

"No, I'm all right. Quite all right, thank you."

"You need a drink. Come into my office."

Following with reluctance, Frederick glanced hurriedly around the cityroom. It was obviously empty. He was relieved when Durant switched on the lights in his office, brought out a squat brown bottle. The everyday actions seemed to lend reason to a macabre experience.

"This girl reporter of yours," the lawyer said casually, "I must confess it gave me quite a shock."

Durant nodded gravely and said with some sadness, "I just saw her...."

In the slight pause, Frederick died a thousand times.

"... at the morgue," finished Durant. "That was what delayed me. They telephoned me to tell me they'd found the body and would like me to identify it. An unpleasant experience."

Frederick replied with difficulty, "Yes, it would be. There ... there could be no doubt of the identity."

"None. The fall had not smashed her up as badly as you would think. You will recall that Robert Marchand was quite recognizable. If I remember, you provided the identification upon that occasion." He brought out two thick tumblers. "Say 'when.' I'll never forget her face ... white like the sheet that covered her frail body."

Draining the proffered drink at a gulp, Albert Frederick felt it provide a stimulated return of courage.

He was prepared to even laugh at himself for his fancies. As a man of the world, he should possess more sense. A body in the morgue could not stroll the floors of a newspaper cityroom.

"It's a terrible thing," he told Durant, and then added sympathetically, "Has she any relatives?"

"None. It's very sad. We were all so fond of her. The staff has started a collection to pay for her funeral expenses, but I imagine that there will be insurance policies somewhere. I was always led to believe she had a private income."

"Well, if it is necessary, I would consider it a privilege to contribute."

"Always generous, friend Frederick. Another drink?"

The editor bent over to pour into the glass Frederick held out to him. As he did, Frederick looked through the glass partition into the cityroom beyond. The tumbler fell from his nerveless fingers.

The time he was not mistaken. He was staring at the figure of Mary Roberts, standing half in shadow. The face of the girl was grave, her eyes fixed on him reproachfully.

"No!" he cried out. "No!"

"Albert, what is wrong?" Durant demanded sharply. "You look as though you've seen a ghost!"

Frederick clutched at the editor's hand.

"Durant! Out in the cityroom! What do you see? *Who* is out there?"

The editor turned and followed his old friend's gaze.

"I'm afraid," he answered at last, and somewhat coldly, "that you have been drinking too much. There is nobody out there, nobody at all."

CHAPTER 15

The many friends of Albert Frederick began to look at one another and wonder. Such a brilliant mind! Their looks would say; it's a shame!

For the first time in his career, Albert Frederick faltered in the middle of an important case, his thoughts confused. In place of the stern judge in his robes, he seemed to see the sad, reproachful face of Mary Roberts. It was a trick of the sunlight, of course, and of his sleepless nights and his too-great drinking.

"Would you like to retire, Monsieur Frederick?" asked the judge, an old friend. "I will recess the court for fifteen minutes."

"Thank you, Your Honour," mumbled Albert Frederick through grey lips, and collapsed.

"Rest!" jeered his brain. "What rest is there for you, Albert Frederick?"

After about a week in the hospital, he felt better. He would have liked to consult a psychiatrist, but did not dare, afraid of what terrible secrets he might subconsciously give away. Even the seal of the doctor's silence would not cover murder.

He had not seen Michel Lacoste since the last fateful interview. The newspapers had duly reported that Michel Lacoste, the famous young composer, had re-appeared, claiming a loss of memory. Lacoste had produced a letter he said he had taken from his wife's pillow on the night of her death. Police said the letter completely exonerated M. Lacoste, and was incontrovertible proof that poor Mme. Lacoste had died by her own hand while of unsound mind. That was, eventually, the verdict of the coroner's court. The public being what it is, the macabre story had stimulated interest in Michel's forthcoming concert, and ticket sales were brisk.

Once Albert had tried to call his protégé but Michel had hung up on him. Albert thought of removing his patronage from the concert, but his vanity would not allow this human move, besides, he had had to pay for the hall in advance.

The lawyer decided to walk home from the hospital. His doctor had ordered plenty of fresh air and exercise and no work. He wondered how he could live without work. If his doctor had been able to open up his mind and read what went on within, what would his doctor have ordered, then? He smiled savagely at the thought, feeling weak but determined. He knew he had lost several pounds since that night in Durant's office, and that his face was shrunken and old. The appearance of youth he had striven so hard to maintain was gone. He was an aged man, burdened with fear.

As he walked slowly along, Albert Frederick's hopes for a return to his normal life grew. He must permit himself no more of those accursed hallucinations.

The street was all but deserted. A horse-drawn wagon clopped by. An ancient taxicab wheezed out of hearing. It was as quiet, he thought, this empty street, as the grave. The cliché bothered him. The huge bulk of the Ursulines convent was on his right.

Then he saw her. She came unexpectedly, fearsomely, from a side street, striding along freely in the sunlight, and he was struck in his tracks for a moment of pure horror. Recovering, he ran after her, calling her name, but his pace was slow because of his illness. He felt that if he did not catch her, he would surely die.

"Mary Roberts!" he shouted "Mary Roberts!"

The figure of the girl increased its brisk walk. He

found himself sweating in the cool atmosphere. His tongue was clogged against the roof of his mouth. His heart was trying to tear itself through his shrunken chest.

He covered his fevered eyes with his hands, as he ran. When he took his hands away, the figure of the girl was still there. He glimpsed her turning in at a small gate.

"Mary Roberts!" he called again, and his echo from the wall of the convent mocked him.

Albert Frederick tottered through the gate. He was gasping for breath. His face was streaked and grey, his jaw set like a dog holding a stick.

He found himself in a bare antechamber. Its only adornment was a crucifix. Across its short length was a heavy door. Frederick tried it, found it locked. As he shook dementedly at the door-handle, a voice behind him said reprovingly, "Sorry, sir, this is a convent. Men are not admitted."

The half-mad lawyer whirled. In the right-hand wall was a small shutter-window. Through this window gleamed two impersonal eyes.

"Please," he said, catching and holding onto air like a fish swallowing water, and letting it go in little gasps, "the lady–the lady who ... just went ... in ... all I want is some ... information ... please!"

The voice behind the eyes said politely but sternly, "I'm sorry, but we don't give information."

The Judas' Eye banged shut. The convent was blind again, shut off from the world and its woes. Frederick ran, choking, from the empty room into the empty street and back to his empty life.

I saw her, he told himself. I am certain I saw her. But how could she walk through a locked door? Only spirits ... He shuddered. As a materialist, he could not believe, nor could he foreswear his own eyes.

"Anything the matter, sir?" asked an official voice, and he looked up, blinking in the sunlight, into the sternly enquiring eyes of a policeman. "Oh, it's you, Monsieur Frederick! Are you ill?"

"How—long have you been here officer?" he demanded hoarsely.

"Why, right along, sir. I saw you run in the convent there and—"

Frederick clutched his arm in a frenzy.

"The girl!" he almost shouted. "The girl who walked up the street, and ran in ahead of me."

The policeman was puzzled.

"Girl, Monsieur Frederick?" He took off his high helmet and scratched his close-cropped head. "Well now, I don't know what you mean. There wasn't any girl. I particularly remarked you were on the street alone."

Albert Frederick moaned, swayed.

"Get me a taxi, get me home," he whispered through cracked lips. "Get me home!"

The policeman nodded, not taking his eyes from this prominent citizen. For a lesser man, he would have called the patrol-wagon; for Monsieur Frederick, he hailed a passing taxi.

"Take this man home," he told the driver loudly. "And call a doctor. He's seeing things."

After the doctor had gone, Albert Frederick looked at the sedative that had been left for him. He turned the glass around and around in his hand. Thus had poor Blanche Lacoste … …

There was something he had to find out, before he could sleep. What was wrong with him, a doctor could not cure. Only Time had deadened the cancer of his brain that had been left by the murder of Robert Marchand. What could erase from his tortured mind the phantom of Mary Roberts?

He must find and face up to whatever it was that was haunting him.

When he rang the bell at Mary Roberts' apartment,

he did not know what to expect. He whipped his tortured mind to fear the worst. There was silence within, and then the sound of stealthy footsteps. He had turned to run, when the door opened. In the sudden patch of light, a fat, jolly man stood there, smiling.

"Yes, sir," asked the fat man, "what can I do for you?"

"Mlle. Mary Roberts–" Albert managed to croak.

"Oh yes, come in, come in. Sad, very sad. Too bad. A friend of hers?"

"In a way, yes."

"I had to move in right away. The housing shortage, you understand."

Frederick's eyes roamed the apartment relentlessly.

"She–she hasn't been back?"

"How do you mean?" The fat man's little eyes took in his haggard visitor suspiciously. "Of course she hasn't been back! What a cruel thing to say about someone buried more than a week! I can't understand you, Monsieur, nor why you should talk like that."

Frederick drew a shaking hand over his eyes.

"I–I'm sorry," he stammered. "The–the shock … I–I–"

He could not go on, but turned and walked away on trembling legs. The shadows closed around.

The thunderstorm was accompaniment to Albert Frederick's horror. His whole world had tumbled about him. He had to believe that he was haunted while his whole thinking and training scoffed at such a notion.

Mary Roberts had gone to her death. The newspapers had proclaimed it. Michel Lacoste's unalterable enmity had told him that. Durant had confirmed it. Yet on three separate occasions since her death, he and he alone had seen Mary Roberts. He had been able to conquer Robert Marchand, to forget about Renée

144

Brancourt, to feel pity for the Lacostes. But Mary Roberts refused to die!

The lawyer poured himself another drink. He knew he was drinking too heavily, but it brought him a certain amount of forgetfulness. The price would be heavy, but he, who had always been a moderate drinker and an advocate of temperance, was prepared to pay that price.

He brought the drink to his lips, when it froze there. A brilliant flash of lightning had lit his window like day and gone, but on his brain was still imprinted the sight he had seen: the face of Mary Roberts, streaming with rain and staring at him with mute appeal. Gripping the tumbler, he stared fixedly at the window-pane, waiting for it to light again. He had not long to wait. The lightning revealed nothing unusual, and he relaxed slightly. It was all imagination. He would have to get over this, prove to himself that he was still a civilized man far removed from the grip of primitive fear.

The glass was to his lips again, when the next flash of lightning etched the face of the girl he knew to be dead. With a hoarse growl of animal fury, he leapt to his feet, and threw the glass with all his force at the pane. Both shattered into fragments. He leaned through the broken edges. The rain beat against his face.

There was nothing but the whipping branches.

Fog hung the cemetery in shrouds, so that Albert Frederick had difficulty in finding his way. A bribe to the lodgekeeper had told him where he would find Mary Roberts' grave.

"A purty young miss," that old man cackled. "Too bad about her. Too bad."

"You– you buried her?"

"I saw to the job." The old man had laughed again.

"When I puts 'em down, they stays down. You sure you want to go down there alone at three in the mornin'? It's agin all the rules."

"I'm quite sure," Frederick had answered stiffly. "And I've paid you well to forget about it."

The lines on Frederick's face were as deep as the night, his thoughts as black as the tunnel of dripping trees into which he plunged. His flashlight dimly picked out the names on headstones. He went from one to the other methodically, disregarding those that were obviously old. Finally he stood over a brand-new stone that said:

MARY ROBERTS
Born May 19, 1923
Died October 23, 1946.

The light picked out the lines of a fresh-dug grave. The flowers on it were withered. Grass had begun to sneak in around the edges. It had not been disturbed. He dropped to his knees, as he had not done since he was a child.

Something forced him to look up. As he did, he gave a startled cry.

The figure of Mary Roberts was standing, half-hidden by the fog, motionless beside a nearby tree. The face was as still as death, the eyes accusing.

With an inhuman scream, Albert Frederick leapt to his feet and ran blindly in the opposite direction. He collided with something that yielded and screamed again. Arms went about him.

"What's the trouble, Albert?" asked Michel Lacoste.

"You!" croaked Frederick, when he could get his breath. "What are you doing here?"

The composer glanced sadly towards the grave of Mary Roberts.

"The same thing as you, I imagine," he answered hollowly.

"Then—then you, too, see her?"

Michel nodded miserably.

"Killers are haunted, Albert. I never believed it, but now I know. Every day ... every night ... in the street ... in my room ..." Michel covered his face with his hands. "It is too much! And it's all your fault."

"Please! I'm suffering, too." Finding Michel in distress had strengthened Albert Frederick. "But we must get over it, perhaps together."

"Never! I want nothing to do with you ... murderer!"

"Once again the pot and the kettle." The lawyer failed in his attempt to lighten his voice. His eyes were darting fearfully to each shadow, to each wisp of fog. "There are no ghosts, Michel! There are hallucinations. They will pass. It's all in our minds."

"People have been driven out of their minds," Lacoste answered somberly.

"Don't talk like that!"

"Sometimes I wonder whether the noose is not better than the straitjacket."

"Stop it!" Frederick tried to shake his companion but had no such strength left. "There is no such thing as a ghost; no such thing!"

His wild, hysterical laughter was enfolded by the arms of the fog that hung over the cemetery. Then, running, stumbling, falling, running again, Albert Frederick left that accursed place and that accursed man. Even his shrieks of insane laughter were finally swallowed up by the dreariness of the cemetery.

A finger of fog touched the gravestone of Mary Roberts with a tear.

CHAPTER 16

Outside the cemetery, an automobile was parked. It was Mary Roberts' car. Michel Lacoste walked over to the car, climbed behind the wheel. His face was white and grim. The scene in which he had acted had left him greatly shaken. After all, at one time he had thought Albert Frederick the finest man in the world....

The shadow beside him moved, stretched, yawned.

"For a ghost," said Mary Roberts, "I'm terribly hungry."

The composer switched on the dashboard, stepped on the starter. As he looked at the girl, beside him, the grimness was wiped magically from his face, leaving him young and boyish. He laid his hand on her very corporeal arm affectionately.

"I hope it hasn't been too hard for you, Mary," he said.

"It hasn't been easy, Michel, particularly this last." She sighed. "But it's in a good cause."

"I've never seen such a change in a man." Michel slid the motor into second gear noiselessly. "When you first outlined your scheme, I could not believe a man of Albert's intelligence would fall for such tomfoolery."

"It's his conscience doing the work. He's lived with a guilty conscience, now, for twenty years."

They drove along the cemetery road and out onto the highway in a comfortable silence. These last days had drawn them very close together. Mary snuggled up for warmth.

"Tell me, Michel," she said slowly. "I've never asked

you until now, but tell me, what *did* you intend to do on the top of Montmorency Falls?"

"I don't know," he confessed. "I really don't. I suppose Albert Frederick had sold me so much to the devil that I intended to go through with it. Besides, I was angry with you about the gun. But then when I grabbed you and you screamed, I wanted to hold you rather than push you. Let's not talk about it anymore, shall we? It gives me goose-pimples to think of it!"

She laughed, and it was a happy laugh.

"You're brave and free and kind," he told her. "I can't have you taking any more risks with that man. Anything might happen. Weren't you frightened just now, when he screamed?"

"No," she said simply, "not with you around."

"Thanks," he replied, his eyes on the road.

Inspector Renault had lost some of his habitual calm. He paced up and down the narrow interrogation-room, his eyes snapping and his moustache half into his mouth.

"I should never have let you and those two young fools talk me into this mad venture!" he stormed at Edward Durant, who was sitting straddle-legged across a wooden chair contentedly smoking his pipe. "It's as much as my job is worth, if I'm caught in a thing like this against a prominent citizen like Frederick."

"Take it easy, Renault," Durant said placidly. "*L'Information* is not without its influence, either. Eh, Lafont?"

"Lafont" was the little fat man who had answered the door to Albert Frederick when the lawyer had called at Mary Roberts' apartment. He had been whispering to the policeman who had not seen anyone but Frederick go into the convent, but he jerked his head up when he heard his name and smiled politely.

"I wouldn't worry too much about them," said Lafont. "Cadieux and O'Reilly are trailing them, and they'll see they come to no harm."

"Sure, chief," agreed the policeman.

A moment later Mary Roberts and Michel Lacoste walked into the room. The Inspector sat down abruptly.

"At last!" he said.

"We had to trail him to the cemetery," said Mary.

"The cemetery!" Durant took his pipe out of his mouth. "What in the world would a man like that be doing in a cemetery?"

"He wanted to look at my 'grave.'"

"Oh. An artistic job, that. Murderers, it seems, are always haunted."

"I wish you'd been there, Inspector."

"Why?"

"To arrest him. He's ripe for a breakdown."

"Arrest him?" barked the Inspector. "Arrest him for what? Have I a single piece of evidence against this man, one of the biggest men in Quebec City? Can I build up a case that will hold water for even the dumbest jury in the province? What have you given me? A diary? Without substance! If there were any clues in it, their trails have been skilfully erased over the years."

"What about the doodle?" asked Mary, somewhat discouraged.

"Pooh! Thousands of people doodle with matches."

"Well, how about his asking me to 'eliminate' Mary?" put in Michel.

"It's your word against his."

"You see," said Durant consolingly, "what the Inspector is up against. Albert Frederick is highly respected by everyone. I even counted him as a good friend. He's generous ... charitable ..."

Michel cut in bitterly with, "He bought himself influence with money stolen from a man he murdered.

Then he was willing to have murder done again, when he thought himself discovered."

Inspector Renault banged the table with his fist. "That's why I'm going to get him!" he promised. "I want to prove that in my city nobody, no matter how important, can get away with crime."

Durant nodded virtuously.

"That's why I printed a false piece of news in my paper for the first time in my life." He added as an afterthought, "Consciously, that is."

Spreading his hands on the table, Inspector Renault looked over the dejected assembly.

"We are not beaten, yet, my friends! The poison is working. As long as Albert Frederick does not discover he is being tricked, as long as he thinks he is being haunted by the dead, there is a chance he will crack and spill everything." A plain clothes man came in and waited respectfully for his superior to notice him. "Yes, Larry, what is it?"

"It's Mr. Frederick, sir," reported Larry. "He's booked a seat on the night plane."

Inspector Renault jumped up, rubbing his hands together.

"Ah, it still ferments!" he cried.

"But he intends to go to Mr. Lacoste's concert beforehand," the detective concluded.

The Inspector thought for a moment.

"We can't let him get to the States," he said. "That would mean extradition, and what proof have we that would call for such a move? Couldn't we do this? It's one of those 21-passenger planes, I'm sure, and has a washroom. Mary could hide in the washroom until the 'plane was aloft then come out. At several thousand feet, that should do the trick!"

"It's too great a risk!" said Michel Lacoste.

"She'll be well protected."

"I hope it works," said Durant dubiously. "Personally, I think Albert Frederick will see through it."

"That's because you haven't seen Frederick in the last little while. I tell you, you'd hardly know him. It's as though he'd been in prison for twenty years. Now, why did I say that?"

"I hope it's my last appearance as a ghost." Mary sounded plaintive.

"Well," smiled the Inspector, "until 'plane-time, you shall have a holiday."

Mary went over and took Michel's hand.

"I was so afraid I was going to miss the concert," she said. "I have a new evening dress I'm dying to have you see."

"Here, what's this?" cut in the Inspector, before Michel could speak. "Who said you were going to any concert?"

It was too much for the girl.

"I'm sick of being a ghost!" she raged. "I'm sick of staying in the house! I want to hear Michel's concerto."

"Use your head, girl!" said Durant impatiently. "Didn't you just hear the detective say Frederick will be there?"

"All right, I'll be inconspicuous. I'll go as a mouse. I won't wear any evening dress."

Inspector Renault liked such stubbornness only in himself.

"See here, young lady, you'll stay away from the concert, or I'll lock you up as an accessory after some fact or other!"

"We need a holiday, too, Miss," said Lafont placatingly.

"You were lucky the last time," growled the Inspector, with a glance at Michel. "The next time—"

He ran his finger over his throat and made a horrible sound.

"You don't want to endanger Michel's concert, do you?" asked Durant.

This last argument was effective with Mary.

"All right," she said resignedly, "only I *did* want to hear the concerto so much."

"That will be very easy, mam'selle." Lafont smiled his fat little smile. "The concert is being broadcast. You have a good radio in your apartment."

"But–"

"Frederick has already been to the apartment looking for you. The chances are a thousand-to-one against his returning."

"He's right, Mary," said Durant.

Mary nodded and went over to Michel Lacoste. She held out her little hand firmly.

"Good luck," she said.

It was cozy to be back in her apartment on the roof of Quebec. Mary Roberts realized, now, how she had missed it. She drank in the view for the hundredth time, watching the winking harbor lights and feeling herself on a magic carpet while her city sped beneath her to the sea.

"Whisper, city," she said to the night. "Whisper! Is it real this time, or is it just another dream? Let it be real, city, let it be real!"

As she realized what she had said, she flamed fiery red and turned from the window. Her white negligée clung to her lovely body, accenting her youthfulness and charm. She went to the piano, and began running up and down the scales, knowing everything was aimless because her life was pointed towards eight-thirty and a concert.

The doorbell rang, and she gave a little scream. When it rang again, she called out, "Who–who is it?"

"Michel!" answered a well-remembered voice.

She flung the door open joyfully.

"This is a pleasant surprise, Michel!"

He was embarrassed.

"I had a couple minutes to spare, and I thought–"

Mary asked eagerly, "What?"

"I tried to think of a good excuse to see you before the concert." He chuckled. "I couldn't find one."

"As if you needed one! Come in and take off your coat. I'll mix you a drink."

"I'm afraid there isn't time. I mustn't miss the opening of the concerto. That would not be right."

"Of course, it wouldn't! You needn't stay a moment past when you feel you should go."

"I would like to stay, Mary."

Her brown eyes flew open wide.

"Oh?"

"Yes. You see–" He groped for words. "This room ... even the first time I came I thought of–"

"Of what?"

"Well, have you ever felt when you saw a place for the first time that you know it, although you're sure you've never seen it before?"

"It could have been a dream."

"Yes." He looked at her fully, and she could see his lower lip was trembling slightly. "Yes, it could have been a dream, an old and wonderful dream ... peace ... cheerfulness ... home ..."

"Was the dream a lonely one, or was it shared?"

He thought how her eyes outshone the stars.

"It was shared," he said shortly, then looked at his watch to break the spell deliberately. "It's time for me to go."

"Wait! Michel, am I so hateful?"

The young man turned away, his face a mask of hurt.

"Don't ask," he said huskily. "You know why."

"It's in the past!" Mary cried. "It's done!"

He continued towards the door. Trying to hide her depression, she gestured towards the radio and told him, "My seat for the concert ... front row, center."

At the door he hesitated, fumbling for words.

"May I–may I come back when it's over?" he blurted out.

"Oh, will you?"

"Right after the finale," he promised, edging out the door.

"This is for good luck," she said, and, leaning forward, kissed him on the cheek.

It was the spark to the tinder. All the pentup longing of the nightmare days now past was in the strength of Michel's lips as he kissed her. She responded with passion too long dormant. Abruptly he let her go and turned his head away.

"I'm sorry," he muttered. "I shouldn't."

She stopped his words with tender fingers.

"Shhh ... let me do the talking. I know how you feel. I understand. But some day ... well, someday you'll put your bad memories behind you. Then– you must say to me all the nice things you can't say now. Remember them, every single one of them, for me ... darling ..."

He went without a backward glance, but there was new and bounding life in every step he took. Mary Roberts closed the door, walking into her bedroom, and took her brand-new evening gown from the rack in the closet.

She would wear it to the concert, anyways, for him.

Montmorency Falls, she told herself with gladness, was a million light years away.

CHAPTER 17

The music flowed through the loudspeaker, filling every corner of the heart of the woman who listened. Mary Roberts was breath-taking in her white evening gown that set off perfectly her flawless brunette beauty. She listened with parted lips and shining eyes to the music of the man she loved.

How had she come to love this man, her thoughts kept time with his music? Once, he had had murder in his heart for her. Twice, an infinitesimal leaning the other way might have brought about her death. Now she was wholly his, if he would have her. Was it because of his music? That was it, partly, but mostly it was because of him. Life had not been kind to him, but she would make that up and erase all the bad memories.

Mary Roberts wrapped the music about herself like a warm, bright blanket, and was happy.

She did not hear the creak of the door to the kitchen, she was so absorbed. It was a sixth sense warned her she was not alone. She looked up, paralyzed with fear.

Albert Frederick stood there in contemplation.

The lawyer was shabby and unkempt. He had a two days' growth of grey beard, and his eyes were bloodshot and wild. Yet the music had rooted him to the spot. Then, with the ease of the confirmed concert-goer arriving late, he slid noiselessly to a seat on the couch.

Mary shrank away from him into as small a bundle as she could make, tucking her feet under herself. Her eyes were immovable with terror. She tried to speak, but her mouth only opened spasmodically, and no sound came out.

Frederick put a hand to his grey lips unsmilingly.

"Shhhhhh!" he commanded and leaned forward to give his full attention to the music he had created vicariously.

Seconds passed, and then minutes. Mary Roberts, over her initial fright, began to move stealthily, an eye on the open door. Her intention was to leap and run, slamming the door behind her as she went. Frederick seemed rapt in the music. She gathered herself for the spring.

Her weird visitor thrust his hand in his breast pocket.

"Don't move!" he whispered.

Mary relaxed, discouraged. She could see the bulge of the gun where his hand had been. She watched desperately for another opportunity.

The man seemed completely taken with the music, looking off into space and nodding his head in satisfaction from time to time.

"Delightful! Great!" he murmured at last. "I always knew he had it in him. Michel, Michel, I'll make you the greatest name in the world of music. I'll arrange a tour for you, Michel. That's it! A tour! New York! London! Paris!" He drew a deep breath and gave it out again in a great sigh. "Tonight–tonight I shall be able to sleep."

Albert Frederick, Mary saw with horror, was mad.

"Still too much romanticism in his music," the madman continued his soliloquy, "but also a growing spiritual quality. He can do great things with my help." Suddenly he whipped on the trembling girl, catlike with a mouse. "Why did he have to meet you? Why? You–"

He broke off, put his fingers to his lips again, listened.

"A delightful passage, Mlle. Roberts. Always a favourite of mine from the time he first played the

157

concerto for me on the piano." His voice rose. "I was the first to hear it played, did you know that? Not you, or anyone else, but me, Albert Frederick, patron of the Arts!" His horrible laughter filled the apartment almost to the exclusion of the music. "They think I'm mad. *You* think I'm mad. Only the insane, they say, have hallucinations. Ah, but I have had a hallucination, and I am not insane. I have thought you were dead, but obviously I was wrong. You are sitting there, across from me, afraid ... and the dead have no fear!"

Again the insane laughter was obbligato to Michel Lacoste's inspired music.

"You do not speak? Oh, but you are flesh-and-blood, mademoiselle, and I shall have the pleasure of proving that. And you will soon be really dead, ma petite. Albert Frederick cannot afford to let you live. Do you want to know how I knew you were alive? This brain works to perfection. It has been called the finest in all Quebec. It still works. I saw your car behind the concert hall, Mlle. Roberts. That told me—that told me—"

His voice trailed off. He made a vague gesture.

"I'll remember later. Right now, let's listen!"

The concerto moved majestically to the finale of the first movement. When it ended, the applause crashed on deadly silence in the apartment.

The thunder of applause was music to Michel Lacoste as great as that he had created. But there was praise he wanted above all other, and he hastened to the telephone backstage.

Michel called Mary's number nervously. It rang; he waited.

"The number doesn't answer," sang the operator.

"Try again, please," Michel told her, a constriction about his heart that left it fluttering.

The number rang, then rang again.

"Sorry, it does not answer."

The young man slammed down the receiver, hurried for the stage door.

Mary jumped to her feet when the telephone rang, reached for the instrument. With one hand, Frederick held down the receiver, with the other he reached for his breast-pocket.

"Stay where you are!" he snarled.

The bell shrilled again. Mary retreated to her corner, baffled. She knew it must be Michel calling. He was so close to her, and yet, so far away.

The music of the second movement swelled through the loudspeaker.

It was too much. Mary lost her control.

"What do you want?" she screamed, her voice piercing into the Lacoste music. "You can't possibly want to kill me! You said you're not crazy. You couldn't do anything crazier!"

"Stop talking!" commanded Frederick hoarsely. "I want to listen to the music."

He closed in on her menacingly. She huddled higher on the couch. Words hammered from her, words with which she was trying to beat sense into a madman's brain.

"I can't escape. You said so. If you kill me, that's a confession ... a confession to the Marchand murder."

The killer halted in his tracks. His confused mind tried to cope with what Mary had said. All that he could think of was Robert Marchand, and a dead-white, pleading face upturned to him for half an instant before it was swallowed in the immensity of Montmorency Falls.

"I had a right to kill Marchand," he said, as much to convince himself over the chasm of twenty years as anything. "Who was he? A nobody with too much money he threw away with both hands. In my keeping, this money has been a blessing. It bought beauty like this." He gestured towards the radio. "It will go on working for the best as I decide … I, Albert Frederick …"

His eyes cleared, and he gazed at her with the fearful realization of what he had said. He made a swift movement and caught her. She screamed, but it was lost in the crescendo of the music.

"Now you have my confession! But you're not going to talk!"

Mary struggled with the madman futilely. He was strong with the strength of the insane.

"Wait a second!" she pleaded frantically. "Think! Where is your alibi? They'll miss you at the concert. They'll look for you at once. Think!"

Her back was to the open window. It would work out as he had planned it once before, but this time he had to kill with his own hands. To kill again! His grip faltered momentarily, then took hold with renewed strength.

Mary felt her spine against the sill. She was going back farther and farther. The lights of her city whirled at her from a grotesque, death-dealing angle. The pressure on her back was intolerable. Her slim legs kicked futilely at him, became entangled in the evening gown that was to have been her happiness and now would be her shroud. His hand was pulsing hard against her breasts.

"Think!" she gasped.

"Later." He increased the pressure. "My head will be clearer … much clearer … later …"

Her hands tore at the casing, held on grimly. He panted with effort, drew back a fist to smash in her face, to end it all.

The door to the apartment crashed open under powerful shoulders. Michel Lacoste streaked across the floor. He whirled the mad lawyer around, felled him with one vicious punch to the jaw. He pulled the fainting girl back to safety.

"Mary! Mary!" he cried, holding her tight. "Are you all right, darling?"

She clung to him, unable to speak, her breath coming in great gasps that changed to sobs. They paid no attention to the man on the floor.

It was a mistake. Crazed Albert Frederick had but one idea left in his twisted brain, to kill Mary Roberts. He struggled back from the effects of Michel's blow, forced his hand into his breast-pocket, brought out his revolver, aimed it.

There was a loud report.

Mary and Michel whirled apart. Albert Frederick half-sat, an odd look on his face. Blood trickled from the corner of his mouth. His pointed gun slid down idly, fell on the floor. He was given a moment of sanity.

"Last round to you, Renée," he said, as if to some-one who had just come into the room.

Death rattled in his throat.

Turning towards the door, Mary and Michel saw Inspector Renault blow the smoke from the barrel of his pistol reflectively.

"So you had to take justice into your own hands," Mary whispered.

"Yes," said the Inspector gently, "he must face the highest court, now. And there will be no appeal."

Albert Frederick slept after twenty years.

While the music played, arm-in-arm, Mary and Michel looked out over the city.

The city whispered to them.

What it whispered is another story.

THE END